MOON OVER PORT ROYAL
Horace B. Alexander

This is a fictionalized account of a true event. Any resemblance to actual persons, living or dead, is purely coincidental.

Publisher: Jamcan Publishing
ISBN: 978-0-9989778-0-5
Card Catalogue Number: 2017907367
Title: *Moon Over Port Royal*| Horace B. Alexander
Formats:
Digital distribution | Jamcan Publishing, 2017
Paperback | Jamcan Publishing, 2017

Dedication

To the youth and friends of Jamaica who must not forget this colorful heritage.

CONTENTS

PART ONE

PART TWO

PART ONE

Prologue

In the quiet half-light of the evening a lone figure rode along the Spanish Town Road toward Kingston. The narrow graveled road, barely enough to accommodate the width of a carriage and perhaps an armed escort on either side, was deserted except for a peasant or two with a donkey or mule returning from the open-air market in Kingston. The horse cantered along at a comfortable pace, its rider erect and in a command position atop his mount, with top hat and waistcoat, fashionable breeches and supported by an ornate saddle richly embossed with patterns of paisley.

The crunch-crunch of the horse's hooves on the gravel was a friendly cadence to the evening breeze and the rustle of the trees, but he was alert. This was a prime scenario for a highwayman to strike, or a runaway slave to exact vengeance on a lone traveler. Of this the rider was quite aware.

The Ferry Inn seen from a distance seemed like a scaled-down great house, and deliberately so because it catered to the needs of fashionable travelers between

Kingston and Spanish Town, and to those who found it a convenient rest-stop on their way from Spanish Town past Kingston to Port Royal. The property rested on the bank of a creek and in 1677 its owner, William Parker, had given permission for a ferry to be built to allow travelers to cross from one side to the other. An astute businessman, Parker saw the potential for profit and in 1684 built the Ferry Inn at that strategic spot along the road. The lower level of the inn included some bedrooms and a tavern where the best of Jamaica's travelling society would pause, commiserate, negotiate, and be on their way.

The outlines of the structure became more evident, emerging from the evening mist as the rider approached. Counting the attic, it was a three-level affair that, viewed from the side, revealed a flight of steps of squared cut-stone construction leading to the second level of the structure. Under these steps was an arch serving as the entrance to the ground floor of the establishment where the tavern was located. The steps themselves led to the upper floors, the main reception area of the inn, made of wood and cut-stone and with rooms for overnight stays. A spacious attic added to the room capacity of the inn. From the attic, window boxes protruded out of the roof allowing light and ventilation when in use. The entire compound reminded one of a tropical oasis with tall palm trees silhouetted against the horizon and bamboo trees on the banks of the creek swaying gently with the evening breeze.

"A room please, and provisions for my horse." The white inn-keeper looked up somewhat curiously at the sight of a dark-skinned man dressed in top hat that he removed on entering the establishment, and who, by his every mannerism showed the breeding of a gentleman. Free blacks of various hues from mulatto to very dark were known to exist, but this was the first time he was interacting directly with one.

"Yes, sir. One night, I presume?" The traveler having nodded, the innkeeper put two fingers to his lips and blew a siren whistle that summoned the livery attendant almost immediately to the room. A quick tilt of the innkeeper's head as quickly dispatched him to attend to the horse tethered outside.

"And the name, sir?"

"My name is Bolt. John Bolt."

Bolt was used to the curious looks of people upon seeing such as he. He received his key and went to his room while the innkeeper registered his name.

Once settled in for the night, Bolt opened the back door of his room and saw that it faced the rear of the building, behind the tavern and on the ground floor. He wanted to allow for airing out the room, the smell of stale rum being pervasive, and sat in the darkness on the wooden three-level step that descended to the ground and the bank of the creek. It was time to pause and enjoy the cool of the evening after the ride from Spanish Town and to contemplate the smooth flowing water in the creek with bamboo leaves and the usual flotsam and jetsam that accompanied such streams.

Presently, he recalled having packed both the fife and flute that he carried in his bag along with his grooming kit and a change of clothing. At first he sat on the steps and played the fife quietly, little tunes that recalled his childhood in the great house as a boy servant and later as a bookkeeper. There were the digging songs that slave drivers encouraged the slaves to sing to keep pace with the high production demands of their overseers. These were lively, energizing ditties that paced the work and helped time pass until the next respite. Then there were those haunting, bittersweet songs that wailed and wept through the fife.

He was one of the more fortunate ones. Mother, bless her heart, had been the "bed-warmer" to Busha on a plantation in St. Thomas parish. Busha was a more benevolent backra than others of his ilk of the European vintage. Whether there was love between slave and master was anyone's guess, but the house servant seemed devoted to her master and when the baby boy was born she secured a place for him as a servant boy to help with errands around the house instead of being sent to the backbreaking labor of the sugarcane fields.

He had befriended an old slave who took the young boy under his wings, telling him Anancy stories and other tales from Africa in his broken English. John often stole away from the single room that he and his mother occupied in the basement of the great house to visit his friend in his humble wattle-and-daub hut. John's mother would often send a calabash yabba, filled with some house food for the old man. The old man would bless John for his good deeds in bringing him leftovers and an occasional sugar-head which he used to make sugar-and-water, a welcome treat for a slave at the end of a toilsome day in the cane fields.

One day the old man took a slender bamboo and using a crude old knife-blade that he had fitted with a wooden handle, he carved and bored holes in the bamboo to make a fife. He played some lively and some sad tunes and John, visibly intrigued, asked to learn how to play the fife. The old man obliged, making another fife that he gave to him as a present. Later, when he was trained as a bookkeeper, he bought a proper flute in Port Royal while on a visit, and taught himself how to play it. When the massa died he left in his will that both John and his mother should be freed and

John provided manumission papers ensuring his status as a freedman.

As Bolt began to lose himself in the music of his youth he noticed that to his left a rectangular shaft of light had suddenly appeared on the ground as someone had opened a door. Then a silhouetted figure appeared, and though the ground distorted the figure somewhat, it became apparent that someone had sat down in the doorway. Bolt's room lantern remained unlit, but the person seemed unaware of the shadow being cast on the ground from the lantern in his or her room. Bolt became aware that though he had initially played softly, the volume of his music had unwittingly escalated as he got caught up in the nostalgia of his songs.

Soon, he abandoned his fife for his flute and his musical musings continued unabated, consciously quieter so as not to disturb the tranquility of his neighbor. He recalled some of the songs he learned by listening to the English massa and his guests sing and play on the pianoforte which sat in the drawing room of the great house. As he played, it became apparent that the person had indeed been listening to the music because the figure seemed to lean more toward and against the doorpost in Bolt's direction. As he continued, the head turned and he could see the outlines of abundant hair and the unmistakable facial profile of a woman. The lips were thicker than one would expect of a white woman and the nose rounder, nobler even, but it was hard to know if this was simply distortion of the shadow by the topography of the ground.

He began to play the haunting melody of "Greensleeves." This must have resonated with his listener because she turned even more in his direction, sacrificing the sharp profile of her face and hair, but her action intrigued Bolt all the more. Who was this woman? Chances were that she was not alone in this place. He might inquire of the innkeeper as to who she was, but then maybe it is better to do one's own private investigations.

Suddenly, a second but larger silhouette appeared. There was a distinctive yelp of pain when a stout arm grasped and pulled the first figure by the hair into the room and then slammed the door shut. The shaft of light was gone as suddenly as it had appeared and only an angry muffled male voice remained, punctuated by the high-pitched, painful whimpers of the female. What to do next? Despite the brandings, beheadings, hangings, mutilation and other abuses of slaves, no charges were ever brought against these Europeans, since each planter or overseer was judge, jury, and executioner on his plantation. Still, there must be a way to discover the identity of those two people and who was the brute that so treated a woman.

When he awoke next morning and repaired to the dining room for breakfast, he lingered, furtively observing the few guests to see who might have been the likely characters in the previous night's drama. None seemed to fit the profile. The breakfast of scrambled eggs, breadfruit slices fried golden brown, Johnnie cakes, and pawpaw, washed down with hot chocolate was satisfying. Even the shimmering layer of oil on the surface of the beverage was just like the kind his mother used to make. Breakfast over, it was time to retrieve the horse from the livery stable behind the inn, settle the bill for the care and feeding of the animal, and set out toward Kingston and ultimately Port Royal.

The livery attendant, when asked, had remembered a man and a young woman retrieving their two-wheeled, one-horse trap but had no notion of where the two were headed except for a passing mention of Port Royal. Bolt thanked him and set out on his journey. The morning air was refreshing and invigorating and he sensed the horse's desire to exercise. They broke into a lively gallop down the road bordered with trees, brush, and occasionally a cluster of bamboo. The ride was exhilarating. Sometime later he reined in the horse back from a gallop to a canter because, on rounding a turn in the road, he saw ahead of him a two-wheeled trap going at a brisk trot. With the canopy deployed it was impossible to see the occupants, but Bolt was intent on finding out their identity.

Resuming a lively gallop, he took but a few minutes to ride past the trap and its passengers, tipping his hat as he rode by. It took one momentary glance to confirm his suspicion: the profile of the woman's face as he rode past was clearly that of the woman whose silhouette he had seen the night before, except that now her hair was sheathed in a scarf tied under her throat. The man was a rotund red-necked backra with a wide-brimmed straw hat that obscured his face except for his already sweat-exuding jowls.

Bolt rode on ahead, ever mindful of the party behind him, pondering his next move. Up ahead loomed the imposing figure of a large Ceiba tree. It was a spot where it was customary for travellers to rest a winded horse and enjoy the luxury of the shade provided by wide well-leaved limbs and branches, thick enough to shelter from even the rain which fell on rare occasions.

The cottonwood tree was some twenty feet in diameter and used also as a resting place for slaves and soldiers on long marches. Bolt remembered a local belief that one should never take an axe to a cotton tree, the Ceiba Pentrandra, without first sprinkling white rum, because duppies resided in the roots of cotton trees. At some point during the history of this particular tree some slaves had been hanged from it, and angry duppies haunted the tree. It was almost as wide as it was high, with tall and robust buttress roots that seemed to sweep from the ground upward and become continuous with the lower limbs, the latter so widespread as to extend over the width of the road and form an incomplete arch over the roadway. It was an awe-inspiring life form that defied the passage of the years, and indeed seemed to celebrate it.

Bolt dismounted and waited for the smudge in the distance to more clearly define itself as the two-wheeled one-horse trap approached. He lifted the foreleg of his horse as if to inspect the hoof and shoe, his back toward the approaching pair. He would not reveal his face until that was necessary. The shade of the tree was excellent camouflage for his dark complexion as he hailed the approaching trap which first slowed and almost stopped when upon seeing the horseman more clearly the backra was about to speed up and make a hasty exit, but Bolt tipped his hat and pointed to his horse, and in the most gentlemanly sweep of his arms requested assistance. The trap halted.

"What seems to be the matter?"

"Just a broken saddle strap and a stone

in the hoof. I took care of the latter. Do you perchance have an awl to make a new hole in the leather?" Bolt looked at the woman. A mulatto or white woman with lips swollen on one side and a nasty bruise under one puffy eye.

"So sorry, Mr..."

"Bolt. John Bolt. And how do you do madam?" The fear that paralyzed her was obvious in her face as he tipped his hat.

"Well, we'll be on our way. Good luck."

"Just a moment, sir. I... did address the lady."

"The lady? Her well-being is my concern sir, not yours."

"It is my concern, Sir, when a lady is abused."

"Look Bolt, as one gentleman to another, let this matter rest."

"Gentleman, sir? Surely you are no gentleman to thus treat a woman!"

Bolt looked at the woman. She fixed on him the gaze of her one open eye. The other was dark blue, swollen shut, and reduced to a puffy bulge marked by a dark line of a slit. An almost imperceptible shake of her head said no, do not interfere here. But the pain and fear in her eye...

Bolt had seen that look before. It had been on the faces of slave women when at night a backra reined in his horse outside a slave dwelling and demanded they accompany him to the cane field when the work was over. As a young boy, he witnessed an overseer in a cane field taking a field slave bent over on all-fours from behind, her belly in the late stages of pregnancy reaching almost to the ground. She later lost her baby in a miscarriage. A cavalcade of memories flashed through his mind, of Phoebe who lost an eye to the misdirected tip of a driver's whip, of his childhood playmate Cassie who, though prepubescent, had been viciously violated by a house guest of his master's, her mouth gagged to stifle her screams. The blood rose behind his neck, up to his head, and threatened to lift the scalp. The surging lava of long-boiling anger seemed powerless to contain.

He grasped the leather noseband of the horse. Almost simultaneously the whip lashed out and he felt a sharp sting on his left cheek. He spun around, checking with his finger to see if the skin had been broken, and when he refocused the man had stepped down facing him with a pistol cocked and ready. His other pistol was tucked in his waistband and his left hand was resting on it.

As the man raised his right arm and aimed, Bolt instinctively dropped into a crouch and not a moment too soon for the pistol discharged into the air as he hurled himself at the hulk of a man. The horse, startled by the deafening sound of the pistol, charged forward with the woman, now screaming, still in the trap, and both hurtled forward down the road. Both men staggered, crashing against the roots of the tree, and Bolt for a moment was imprisoned between the tall buttress roots as his assailant pounded his face with his fists. He ducked down and rammed him headfirst in the gut again, propelling both men from between the buttress roots to the ground near where Bolt's horse stood. The hulk of the man fell with Bolt above him as the second pistol discharged, hitting Bolt's horse as Bolt rolled to the side still gripping the man's pistol arm. The horse reared up in alarm and came down with one pounding hoof on the man's head, the other hoof barely missing Bolt himself in the process.

Then there was silence, save for the snorting of the horse, and the rustle of the leaves overhead.

This was not good. The man was clearly dead, the blood seeping out through his nose and mouth and spurting from a nasty gash near his ear. And the only witness was that woman, who now was gone and had heard his name. She had warned by her looks and gesture not to interfere. And the horse was wounded and would survive, but was for the moment useless. There was no means of escape but on foot, and escape was imperative, for no freedman ever brought to trial in the homicide of a

European was ever set free as far as memory served. A public hanging was the inevitable outcome of scenarios like this.

Soon there would be others travelling this road. Think and act quickly. Take nothing from the body, nothing that could incriminate. Extricate the flask of rum which bulged from the back pocket of the dead man and pour its contents on the horse's wounds, return it to the man's back pocket, then slap the horse's hindquarters and send it on its way. It would find its way back to Spanish town from whence it was hired. The saddle would identify the livery stable from which it came.

There was no choice except escape to the hills. Perhaps make his way eventually to Port Royal, mix with the local population and find a suitable pirate ship where one could be free to roam the Spanish Main. Now, in the meanwhile, survive. No family to miss him. Only the place of his employment would be concerned about his absence, his mother having passed away some years earlier. But the death of the backra would be investigated. His name was registered at the Ferry Inn. The livery servant saw him leave. He might recall that Bolt had inquired of the two people in the trap. Then there was the woman. Women can be such unpredictable creatures. What will she say? Where were they going? How will she explain the death of her "master"?

Will she name Bolt? That very uncomfortable, vulnerable, feeling was not alleviated by swallowing the big lump in the throat. His breath was suddenly shallow and short. Too many variables beyond control. But one must survive, and by any means necessary. The hills. Escape to the hills. Now.

CHAPTER ONE

An Arrival

Commodore Christopher Myngs stepped back from the wheel of the Marston Moor and nodded to his First Mate who assumed control of the frigate. He advanced to the rail of the bridge and reached into his waistband where he had secured the tarnished brass spyglass. As he extended it and trained his sights on the distant shadowy landform, he beckoned to the Reverend Dr. Emmanuel Heath to join him.

"Aye, Reverend. There's your new Promised Land. Look at her now and remember this peaceful and beautiful island of Jamaica. Columbus called her the most beautiful isle that eyes have seen. This may be the last time you see her thus. In the coming weeks and months you would do well to remember her this way. Port Royal will come into focus soon and you will know soon enough why she is called 'the wickedest city on earth.'"

Eyebrows raised, the English clergyman nodded graciously as he accepted and trained the brass tube to scan the horizon:

tall needles of the masts of vessels in the harbor, so many it seemed like a hedgehog on full alert. The harbor was crowded with hundreds of vessels, sails drawn up to crossbeams and gathered neatly like the drapes in a governor's mansion. As the Marston Moor gingerly approached the docks and mooring, the houses emerged more clearly. They were clustered together Liverpool-style and many stone buildings near the water's edge. A fort slid into the line of vision, large cannons trained menacingly to ward off any prospective invader. Heath had been told there were six such forts defending Port Royal from any Spaniard invasion.

His impressions of the West Indies before leaving England did not adequately prepare him for these distinguished brick and cut-stone edifices and two-story houses worthy of London. Some houses were fitted with green jalousie windows or white sash-windows and white doors, or mahogany doors polished mirror-smooth. Around the docks there was a bustling beehive of frantic movement and excitement worthy of a capital. Galleons, frigates, brigantines, and caravels, other ships of various nations under privateer and pirate command were coming and going in non-stop commerce. They brought the best of the world's goods, booty, craftsmen, artisans, prostitutes, brigands, and slaves.

This was no primitive outpost. This was the best and worst of England transported and transplanted across the seas, right in the Spanish Main of the New World. What had he gotten himself into? His bishop said one in every four buildings in Port Royal was either a tavern or a brothel or both and that the challenge was to "serve where the need is greatest." The assignment was not without intrigue and a certain excitement. He wondered what his rectory would look like.

As the Marston Moor approached the docks, Commodore Myngs pointed out St Paul's, an imposing structure, not quite a cathedral, but more than a mere church. This was a tall grey cut-stone structure topped by an inverted V-shaped roof and above it all a tower connected to the side of the building enclosing an impressive entrance with double oak doors. The tower continued upward to include a belfry and a tall steeple stretching heavenward. The walls of the main structure were interrupted by tall arched stained-glass windows reaching from the height of a man all the way up to the upper reaches of the building. The sight of the structure was enough to gladden the heart of any country vicar. Here one would be a key figure in an important territory, Jamaica being the prime revenue generator for the English crown, even more so than the American colonies, not that this mattered to such as he.

Going from the deck to the dock, Heath strolled along the planks, looking back at the ships and forward to the shops. People were dressed in the latest fashions from London. He scanned the crowd, searching the faces for one looking as if he expected him. His footing was unsteady, like a half-intoxicated brigand as he recovered his land legs and the hard earth began to feel less spongy to the step. The tangy saltiness of the air assaulted his nostrils; somehow the smell of the ocean was more intense on land than it had been at sea.

Nearby, flocks of egrets were thrashing about near the water's edge, competing for the scraps of gutted fish as local fishermen cleaned their catch for the market that, from pungent evidence, must be nearby. To his right was, horrors, a pirate swinging by the neck as the wind swayed the corpse, eyes bulging in an empty stare, slowly swaying in the Port Royal breeze from a gallows near the waterfront. It was known that seven killings per night was not an uncommon occurrence during some busy periods in Port Royal. He had been told the hangings were usually for offences against the English crown, usually piracy.

A scan of the crowded dock revealed serious-looking merchants, wearied slaves unloading barrels and trunks, crinoline-clad ladies in white dresses, mulatto and white ladies swishing their way through the crowds with their parasols hovering over them to block out the fierce sun. Dark-skinned freed women called "higglers" maneuvered around freedmen and wended their way about with baskets of ground provisions and fruits for sale. One called out "Buy you sweet sop, mango, guava, apple, guinep, cheap-cheap!" as she nimbly negotiated her way among the crowds, her basket brim-full and balanced precariously on her head with a rolled-up kata acting as a cushion between her head and the basket.

The barefoot slaves were readily recognizable by their dress: rough trousers, some three-quarter length, with a crude sack vest and a straw hat secured on the head by a string that was fastened under the throat. The planters clearly stood out in their white drill trousers with tweed waistcoats and over these were long-tailed coats and feet shod with tall black boots. Their heads were covered with broad hats to keep out the hellish sun. Their attire was obviously intended to trumpet their planter status in spite of the torture of a heat chamber within which they walked. Heath watched them fanning themselves and wiping the poring sweat with ubiquitous handkerchiefs. The entire scene seemed at once to be both strange and familiar, with images of waving palm trees and sandy beaches superimposed on the Thames, the docks, and the seafronts of the English coast.

Two wrinkled and emaciated negroes, arms extended, begged by the dockside, both blind. Heath noticed the skeletal hands of one, sinew and bone indistinguishable, with fused finger joints. Both heads tilted upwards, they engaged each other in short stretches of muffled conversation. Passersby avoided the two, both dressed in torn, ragged clothes and presumably foul-smelling. Occasionally two bits landed in the hands of one or the other, the giver careful not to make contact with the palms as the coins were dropped in. Heath caught sight of a man whose mode of dress suggested some type of overseer as he beckoned to another with a tilt of the head and a crooked, malicious smile. They both approached the two blind beggars and Heath drew somewhat closer to watch the interaction.

"Here. A piece-of-eight. Share between ye. This should take care o' ye for a fortnight, pr'haps a month."

"Tenk you, Massa. Tenk you, tenk you" they offered their effusive duet of gratitude. Heath noticed that the overseer had not given either of the men a piece of eight.

"Mek we go change it, so you can gimme me share."

"Me can give you? Is you get de money from de massa!"

"Me no get none!"

"You liar! You wan' fe gyp me. Is you get de money!"

Heath could barely decipher the substance of this exchange but understood the circumstance. The two overseers had stepped aside to watch the drama unfold. Heath looked on as the men began an animated quarrel which soon escalated to flailing arms as they fought futilely while a crowd gathered round to watch the spectacle of two blind men attempting to fight each other.

The fracas escalated as onlookers urged the men on, people taking sides and giving directions to one or the other, all finding the scene too amusing to ignore. Heath could not appreciate the humor of the situation and turned away. He watched the overseers leave the scene as three red-jacketed soldiers moved in to break up the fight and the crowd.

Finally, a gentleman looking in Heath's direction showed a gesture of recognition. The man was neatly dressed in black gabardine-like trousers with a grey waistcoat topped by a black jacket and crowned with a top hat. He tipped said hat and in raised voice addressed him: "Reverend Heath? I am John White, President of the Colonial Council. Welcome to Port Royal." They shook hands, exchanged pleasantries, and strolled along the dock until they saw the neat cobblestones of Queen Street where an open horse-drawn carriage awaited them. Heath's three trunks with his personal effects had been loaded onto a donkey-cart driven by colored servants and would precede them to the rectory.

"Your rectory is near Fort Carlyle, one of six forts guarding Port Royal." The thought of having a residence near a fort that, under Spanish attack, might come into the line of fire was not a pleasant prospect, but Heath said nothing. The carriage proceeded at a dignified pace down Queen Street as White pointed out various buildings.

"The wooden structures are those built by the Spaniards before good ole England, shall we say, expelled the Spanish back in 1655. Those with the cut stone and the half-timbers are, of course, English and more recent."

The governor's mansion, though unoccupied, was particularly impressive. It was a stately Edwardian edifice that despite the sparse acreage on which it was situated, seemed to belong at the end of the long graveled roadway that one would see on an extensive estate in rural England. John White continued, "Sir Henry Morgan, the infamous pirate and later the Lieutenant Governor of the island, died recently and is buried in the cemetery at St. Paul's. There are those who swear that they see him still restlessly pacing along the docks at night looking out to sea. You will see his grave later. There are also those who say he would have preferred a burial at sea."

John White, sitting to Heath's left, remarked about various places of interest on the left of Queen Street, mostly government offices and compounds such as the customs houses and trade agencies, but Heath could not help looking to his right where there was certainly more excitement. Down one shaded and narrow street was an old pirate lying on the cobblestones, his half-hidden, scruffy face covered with a tri-cornered hat, his chest covered in coarse porcine hair and his bare barrel of a belly rising and falling with each breath. There was an empty rum bottle in his hand, and he was fast asleep, snoring raucously at three in the afternoon.

The rumble of the carriage wheels joined in the cacophony of sound and the voices spilling out through the doors and windows of various establishments. The smell of stale rum mixed with equally stale urine wafted across the nostrils. Down the next cobblestone alley was another brigand vigorously pumping a lithe young Spanish prostitute against the patchy brick wall of a tavern. She was open-mouthed, face tilted upward, her raven-black hair in wild disarray and her skirts hiked up about her waist, while her arms dangled, swinging back and forth with every   impact. They seemed oblivious to the raucous, rowdy shenanigans of feuding drunkards spilling out into the dark alley beside them. It was enough to cause a proper clergyman to hurriedly avert the eyes.

Above the din of riotous debauchery, a gunshot startled both men as they transitioned onto High Street. The smoke had barely cleared from the muzzle of the pistol when they identified the source. A privateer, knife in one hand and pistol in the other, was waving the firearm, herding two other ne'er-do-wells over to join him on the ground where he had planted a newly acquired cask of rum. He was demanding they join him in doing it justice. The gunshot was a warning that his request was an offer for which refusal was not an option. John White urged his dark-skinned and uniformed driver to make haste and pick up the pace lest they be extended the same invitation. Sodom and Gomorrah. Was acceptance of this assignment a wise decision?

The rectory was a modest but substantial structure on a quiet street. The lower elevations showed cut stones and concrete with a short but meandering pathway between well-kept circular rose beds leading to the main door that was recessed somewhat to suggest an atrium with a heavily paneled mahogany door complete with a brass knocker. A slim, elderly black woman with a matronly air answered the door and Heath was introduced to Gatha, the servant who greeted him and White at the door. His predecessor had arranged her freedom from a sugar plantation in the parish of Westmoreland and she had ever since dedicated her life to serving the church in her present capacity.

Gatha's lodging was a simple but clean two-room dwelling with an outhouse at the back of the property. She had easy access to the kitchen separated from the rectory by a short walkway with a corrugated zinc-roofed covering overhead. In the interim before Heath's arrival, it was clear that Gatha had single-handedly kept the rectory in good condition. The dray cart had arrived before their carriage, and the trunks with his personal effects had been transferred to his bedroom. Heath set about unpacking with the help of Gatha who by now was obviously used to such duties. She separated the clothes in need of washing and pressing, and inquired of the reverend as to when he might like his first meal. He was famished and so indicated.

Gatha had prepared a meal in anticipation of his arrival: boiled white yams, roasted plantain, and cabbage seasoned with spices and Scotch Bonnet peppers. With this she had chosen boiled ham and stewed chicken, the latter with a sauce made with eggs and butter. A bottle of Demerara stood waiting in case he chose to indulge a little. It was a simple enough meal, but Heath felt very well pampered and was grateful. He soon discovered that the slivers of Scotch Bonnet mixed into the shredded cabbage were more heat than he could handle, but he was generally quite satisfied. He retired to bed, snug under the coverlet. Gatha had asked if he wanted his mattress warmed with the heated stones ensconced under the bed, held in place by a metal framework. Heath declined and wondered to himself why such a thing would be necessary in such a warm climate.

At first he lay awake listening to the strange sounds of the night as the curtains blew inward and waved soothingly. There was the pleasant sound of tree frogs with their two-tone whistle and the occasional nagging whine of a mosquito but that pesky insect was amply kept at bay by the white mesh canopy that enclosed the four-poster bed. The jalousie shutters were open wide enough to reveal a bright, almost full, moon and there was some comfort in knowing that the same moon, were it not shrouded by London fog, also shone over faraway England.

A wider inventory of the abode could be had the next day in the broad daylight and there would be a visit to St. Paul's as well. Gatha had indicated that a lay preacher had been carrying on the church services as best he could, and the parishioners would be quite happy to have a real Anglican parson back in Port Royal. Heath slept soundly that night, soothed by the sea breeze that wafted through the jalousie windows.

CHAPTER TWO

A Surprise Gift

As the months passed, Reverend Heath grew accustomed to his new surroundings and adjusted to the vibrant cultural milieu that was Jamaica and more particularly Port Royal. The oppressive heat was one issue that took time, his dark heat-absorbing clerical robes prolonging the period of adjustment. At first all his dreams were of himself in Merry Ole England and he would awaken to find himself in Jamaica, and smile to himself that he seemed to be still subconsciously in his native land. Then one morning he announced to Gatha quite enthusiastically that he had had a dream the previous night and lo and behold it was of himself in Jamaica. Gatha listened, smiled, and nodded. She seemed amused, as if remarking to herself how strange these foreigners could be at times.

Heath was puzzled by the strange vernacular that challenged his ear every time a native spoke. He heard African sounds and rhythms, a rapid cadence in the speech patterns, all this tinged with an Irish lilt and occasionally Scottish inflections. This intrigued him, and his study of languages in the seminary further aided in his grasping the tenor of this new mode of expression. Soon he understood that "fe" was "for" but also "to" and "haffe" was "have to" and recognized the penchant for substituting a "d" sound for "th" as in "dat" for "that" and "dis" for "this." Other words were of purely African origin and harder to fathom.

He was especially intrigued with the folk sayings or proverbs which he overheard coming from parishioners who hailed from the rural areas, especially the parish of St Thomas. Although he made no attempt at first to speak the local vernacular, he sometimes found a pleasant challenge in deciphering the nuggets of wisdom encapsulated in these sayings. He started a collection of these, recording each new discovery in a small notebook that he kept with him at all times. He would often ask Gatha, what these sayings meant.

"Gatha, what does it mean when a parent tells a child, 'When the chicken is merry, the hawk is near'"?

"'Chicken merry, hawk deh near' is a warning dat when de child too happy-go-lucky dats when dey get hurt. De hawk kill de chicken when de chicken too happy and not careful."

"All right, then: Every day the bucket goes to the well; one day the bottom will fall out."

"'Ev'ry day bucket go a well, one day de bottom a go fall out' mean tings go on long time, but one day it stop widout warning. It mean when we don' expek, justice can come quick quick!"

"Hmm....That is wisdom! Thanks Gatha."

"Sure ting, Reverend."

Reverend Heath recalled the events of one especially memorable day soon after he arrived in Jamaica. One morning he had opened the front door of the rectory as he was leaving, tripped, and almost fell over a fruit crate placed strategically in his path. Regaining his equilibrium, he bent down to inspect the contents of the crate. Peeling back the floral cloth expecting to see a gift of fruit from a grateful parishioner, he saw to his surprise a newborn, fidgeting baby.

"'Gatha? Come here this minute!"

"Yes, sar. What wrong, sar?"

"Take a look Gatha. What do you make of this?"

"Is a just-born baby girl, sar. Navel string still wet."

"I can see that Gatha. Why is it here?"

"Maybe is one of dem whores on Front Street have de child and don't know what to do wid 'er. Couldn't kill de poor thing, so pretty, so she do de next best t'ing, sar.

Looks like a brown-skin baby, maybe one of them negro whores and a seaman. Who knows? So many of dem here in Port Royal.

"Hmmm. Why me?" The infant, navel cord still dripping, started to whimper.

"In as much as ye have done it onto the least of these..." He recalled being told that John Starr had twenty or more white prostitutes in his "establishment" and two negroes, but similar brothels had whites and negroes, prostitutes of every hue, including that English whore Mary Carleton who ran her own house of ill repute. These brothels offered a wide range of choice to suit every taste. The baby might have come from these or any of numerous other such "establishments" in Port Royal.

"Gatha, I have to be away for part of the day in Spanish Town and then pay a visit to the Stokes Hall estate in St Thomas. Look after the child and when I return we'll decide what to do."

"Yes, sar. Safe trip, sar."

Heath traveled with John White in his carriage driven by a mulatto freedman to the capital. The men conversed as the council president acquainted Heath with the local political landscape while Heath provided the latest information available to him on the developments back in London. He learned of the increasing popularity and prominence of another West Indian planter and his brother, the Beckfords, who owned multiple sugar estates in Jamaica.

Heath was impressed with Spanish Town, the capital. Originally the capital of the island under the Spanish, it was called Santiago de la Vega and later Saint Jago de la Vega before being renamed Spanish Town by the English. Imposing two-story buildings, many in red brick and others with whitewashed exteriors surrounded a large central park. It was a fascinating mix of English and Spanish architecture: arches and colonnades adorned the full length of some buildings in the park. On one side was the Supreme Court building and Parliament House; on another was a guard-post and accompanying arsenal, while on yet another side of the central square were some derelict buildings that added their decayed charm.

The widest building was the old Kings House or Governor's Mansion from the Spanish era. This edifice occupied an entire side of the square. People busied themselves with sundry activities. There were soldiers all decked out in scarlet coats, slaves going to and fro about their masters' business, one-horse kittereens driven by freed people, whites as well as coloreds, and heavy two-horse and four-horse carriages driven by coloreds conveying well-to-do aristocrats.

Now, everyone knew that decisions were made in Port Royal and formalized in Spanish Town, the capital of Jamaica. The Reverend Dr. Emanuel Heath, having satisfied his curiosity with scanning the surroundings, entered the chambers of the Colonial Council in Spanish Town shortly after deliberations began. His friend John White was presiding over the usual disputatious dozen or so members, each impressed with his own self-importance.

"But, honourable sirs, the construction engineers tell us that Port Royal is built on a cay, a mere sand spit heaped up against a coral reef. All that land below High Street is unstable sand. Just two feet down our builders find the water table. The houses are sitting on little or no foundation. The only stable land is north of High Street. We cannot afford to build any more structures on Port Royal. At last count we had more than two thousand structures on a mere fifty-one acres. That is enough!"

"Nonsense! We are talking about one of the best natural harbors in the world, accommodating up to five hundreds ships, and who wants to tell King Charles that his golden purse of the Indies cannot produce more revenue for the English Crown? There is more wealth per capita circulating here than in London for Chrissakes! We must approve additional building permits."

"Heavens man! Port Royal is the biggest city in the Western Hemisphere, larger than Boston in the American colonies. We do not need to be any larger. I say let us put a freeze on building!"

"Gentlemen! Gentlemen!" John White tried to restore some semblance of parliamentary procedure. "We have quite recently approved twenty additional tavern licenses without additional buildings. These are cottage industries. Every other household it seems is now doubling as a tavern, so revenues can be increased without additional buildings. The current motion is tabled for consideration at a later date."

Down came the presidential gavel.

"Now, as to the matter of the complaints by some citizens of the carousing, gambling and debauchery attendant on the arrival of each new pirate or privateer vessel, what say ye?"

A sudden cacophony of clamoring voices erupted from around the circular table as White struggled to maintain decorum.

Reverend Heath had seen and heard enough. He by now could divine that these complaints would be entertained merely to mollify the interests of a few who did not stand to profit from the emptying of the pockets of the sailors, pirates and privateers as they returned to port with their booty. Port Royal was the only place to spend their ill-gotten gains, and the merchants in the city had far too large a stake in emptying those pockets. They did not mind a few gunfights, knifings by cutthroats in gambling disputes, or the comforts of the numerous brothels welcoming seamen long deprived of female companionship. Heath stepped outside the chambers and awaited the end of the meeting when his friend John White would meet him before his departure to the Stokes Hall Estates.

A firm of solicitors in Montego Bay managed the property, but Montego Bay being on the other side of the island, Lord Stokes had requested of Heath to also keep an eye on how things were going on the estate and the solicitors and the local overseer of the estate were aware of the arrangement. Heath considered this responsibility, a favor to a friend, as an unsavory obligation he begrudgingly fulfilled. The specter of inflicting human bondage for the sake of filthy lucre went against all notions of human decency although there too was conflict because the institution of slavery was not only condoned in Scripture but also endorsed. That much was clear, but this was a moral dilemma, a very personal internal struggle that had been ongoing for some time.

As Heath returned to Port Royal after his visit to Stokes Hall, he realized that brief though the visit had been, it was an experience that left a deep impression, an assault on his sensibilities: the back-breaking labor of humans treated as beasts of burden as the juggernaut of slavery ground on. Heath felt powerless to stop it. What he saw was revolting and yet he felt somehow complicit in its perpetration.

A lifetime of memories, of recalled conversations, of polite banter at high teas in many drawing rooms in so many English manor houses and castles yielded references to Jamaica and to the stories and anecdotes that might give him perspective on his new context of service. Very rarely were there conversations regarding any debt owed to "the colonies" for furnishing the lavish lifestyles enjoyed by the English aristocracy. Instead, there was a mindset of entitlement, a "given" that this was the reward for innate superiority affirmed by right of conquest.

There were some references to someone being "as rich as a West Indian planter" but otherwise "the colonies" were very far away geographically and indeed psychologically. Only the lower echelons of English society who became bookkeepers, overseers, clerks, and indentured servants would have any close encounter with the system. For these people it was both a scourge and a limited opportunity.

Private conversations with the young Lord Stokes (Lord Stokes, the elder, was by this time deceased) had lent him a deeper insight into the psyche of one of those "rich West Indian planters" than was afforded through polite conversations in the drawing rooms of the rich. They lent a perspective that was abrasive to his Christian sensibilities. They revealed a disdain for the natives, free or slave, and the slave trade in general as a necessary evil. His fellow Englishmen at the same time held a deeply felt fear that the slaves and the trade would both turn on the planters in a sudden and devastating counterforce that would destroy the very fabric of the English class system. Fear and disdain could only be controlled by force and savagery. That much was clear to Stokes and others of the English middle class and aristocracy.

In England, Heath recalled, theologians were still debating whether women had souls. How much less would these natives be considered creatures worthy of that privilege? Already the Quakers and other religious groups in England were advocating the abolition of slavery much to the dismay of many who saw sugar and slavery in the West Indies as their only means of access to the English upper classes.

Upon his return late that day Heath and Gatha discussed the matter of what to do with the child. It was agreed they would keep her as part of the household and that once she "passed the worst" as Gatha stated it, she should be sent to serve in the household of a planter. She was not to remain in Port Royal. It was Gatha's job to train her as a servant for a massa yet to be determined.

"She goin' need a name, sar."

"What do you suggest, Gatha?"

"Why not call her Poincie, sar?"

"Poincie? Nice sounding name, but what does it mean?"

"Is short for poinciana, sar, a lovely tree."

"Very well then. Poincie it is. Isn't there a Poinciana tree in the yard at St Paul's?"

"Yes sar, a tall lovely tree. Is a custom here on de island to plant a tree for a newborn child, sar. Is all right if I plant a poinciana in de backyard?"

"Certainly. We could use more shade."

Little Poincie brought some measure of joy to the Heath household, her amusing behaviors and childlike innocence inspired many sermons delivered at St Paul's as Heath drew object lessons from her antics and general development while never naming her. The reverend became quite fond of the little girl, and seeing her natural intelligence, began to teach her to read and write using copybooks sent from England. He allowed her free range in the house whenever she came to the house with Gatha from the humble maid's cottage at the back of the property. He allowed her to borrow books from his library and she sometimes read the Bible and other books to Gatha before going to bed. Heath derived considerable pleasure in seeing her grow and develop into a comely young woman, like the daughter he never had.

Heath noticed that Gatha would often get ground provisions for the house from a young man named Kwaku who came through the side gate of the premises to the back window of the kitchen each week. He called his donkey Calypso. Heath remembered the name Gatha and Poincie had used for Kwaku's donkey and was amused at the very notion that a donkey would have a name, but it seemed within the personality of the amiable Kwaku to do such a thing. He had met him coincidentally on a few occasions as Kwaku did his rounds and the two had merely exchanged pleasantries.

"Calypso." What a name for an ass. Of course the scriptures had that wonderful story of Balaam's ass that had an interaction with an angel, an experience that Balaam, a prophet, was too stupid to engage in. What an irony! But Calypso...Hmmm. That was another story entirely, coming from Greek mythology. Heath resolved to refresh his mind of the story of Calypso. The rectory dictionary showed the meaning of the word: "Calypso:

to cover, to conceal knowledge, to hide." Kwaku would have had no idea what the name of his jackass meant. How could a common laborer know anything about this? "Calypso." A cause for a jolly good laugh indeed. When he returned to England he would certainly mention a jackass named Calypso among the many stories he would tell of his time in Jamaica.

CHAPTER THREE

Kwaku

Kwaku enjoyed the time spent with Poincie and Gatha when he came by the house. He would greet them with, "Hi Miss Gatha" and to Poincie with "Hi Putoos!" a term of endearment Poincie pretended not to appreciate, but her half-smile would tell him she didn't mind at all. She also playfully greeted his donkey Calypso that carried two large hampers, one on each side laden with his wares. The hampers were held up by ropes looped over the protruding ends of an x-shaped wooden frame resting lengthwise on the donkey's back and secured by a rope or strap which went under its belly.

Kwaku, who seemed to favor various shades of green in his clothing, was in his twenties and very strong. His shoulders looked like ridged cabbages, his arms like stout yams and his back had a deep groove down the middle. After his trip down from the hills, he was sweaty and his dark brown skin glistened like Vaseline in the midday sun.

On one of his weekly visits Kwaku chatted with Poincie and Gatha who gave a good report of the Reverend Heath's treatment of them. No, neither the owner nor the overseer of the nearby Stokes Hall Estate had visited Reverend Heath, but Mr. White had been by the house a few times. No, there was no talk of any slave rebellion although it was generally known that Heath didn't look too favorably on slavery.

Poincie ventured to ask Kwaku about his people way up in the hills. Kwaku felt he could trust the young girl and confided in her.

"All right. So, how come you so different? You not a slave like dem over at Stokes Hall Estate dat we hear about. You free. How come?"

"Me modda wuk nuff nuff years fe mek sure me free."

"So she free too?"

"She did free, but she dead now."

"And you fawda? Him free too?"

"Him did free too, but him dead now too."

"So you have brodda or sista?"

"No. Is me one. I wear de good clothes so nobody will tink I am a slave, and I always carry me freedom paper wid me anywhere me go."

"So you cultivate an live way up in de hills?"

"Yes, I am a free man but I choose to live up in de hills near Maroon country. Me live like Maroon, but I don' let too many people know bout dat. It not safe. Keep dat between me and you."

Kwaku sensed the excitement in Poincie when she heard he might know some Maroons, the feared but admired freedom fighters of the Cockpit Country and other areas of the rugged Jamaican highlands.

"So, you like dem?"

"Dem all right but betta no form-fool wid dem."

"Dem really different from we?"

"Yes, Maroon is different. Dem don' tek no crap from nobody!" Kwaku's eyes flashed a piercing intensity that Poincie had never noticed before. "Dem never bow de knee to de white man. Dem is free!!

"So Maroons is not a church?"

"No, but dey have certain t'ings dey believe."

"T'ings?"

"Like the fact dat dere is two kinda people in the worl': dose that treat the earth like a whore and dose that treat the earth like our modda."

"Who treat the earth like a whore?"

"All the pirates, buccaneers, privateers and all dose that encourage them. Like the King of England and Spain and the Dutch. They rape and tek advantage of de earth. The earth is a whore fe dem."

"But Maroons different?"

"Yes. The earth is our modda. We treat her wid nuff nuff respek. But Maroon can't cultivate de earth like everybody else, because doh we live off the earth we can't let the Spaniards or the English find we in the hills. No big plantations or fields. We have fe cultivate de ground provision and crop we can hide under de bush dem."

"But how do you cook in de bush? Don't the white soldiers dem see the smoke?"

"Dats why Maroon cook in the ground on pimento wood, cover up and cook for a long time. Almost no smoke. We cook hog, fowl, and other meat, all slow and spicy. We call it Jerk. I bring you some one o' dese days."

So Mas Kwaku, please tell me one Anancy story before yu go.

Kwaku scratched his head, smiled at Gatha who was watching with a smile while she continued to work but missing not a word of the exchange. Kwaku began:

"One day Brer Anancy decide fe cook stew peas fe de pickney dem. Him season it up and put in all kinda spice and peppa just enuf fi mek it taste and smell good. So Brer Parrot up in de tree smell the pot and decide fe tief some. When Brer Anancy not looking, Parrot drop down and scoop up some in a leaf and swallow it quick time. Den him fly back up inna de tree, all pleased wid himself. Nex ting yu know him wiggle him batty because the peppa bu'n him backside. So Parrot sing:

'Stew peas, stew peas, sweet like Natty,
Full yu belly, but bu'n yu batty!'

Brer Anancy hear Parrot and realize what happen. Brer Anancy know dat Parrot talk too much so he know soon everybody will know 'bout the stew peas. Next come Brer Dog. But Anancy was ready fi him. He put extra pepper inna de pot and watch wha happen. Brer dog tief some a de stew and run off feelin' pleased wid himself. Him swallow de stew peas quick quick. Then next ting yu know Brer Dog drop down pon him backside and a skate pon him ass on de grass wid him back leg dem cocked up, 'cause him batty a bu'n him real bad! So Parrot sing:

'Stew peas, stew peas, sweet like Natty,
Full yu belly, but bu'n yu batty!'

Den come Brer Tiger. Dis time Anancy really pepper the stew peas and hide behind a tree fi watch wha happen. Brer Tiger swipe a few mouthfull a de stew, swallow it down real quick and take off feelin' pleased wid himself. Next ting yu know he run down to the river, lift he tail up high wid he ass in the wata sayin 'cool it wata, cool it; cool it wata, cool it!' And Parrot sing:

'Stew peas stew peas, sweet like Natty,
Full yu belly, but bu'n yu batty!'

From dat day on nobody bodder Brer
Anancy and him stew peas afta dat."

They all had a healthy laugh and Kwaku felt
flattered that Poincie so eagerly wanted to
hear his words, his stories, his views.

Chapter Four.

Poincie

When Kwaku left that day Gatha engaged in pressing the laundered clothes, all the while reminiscing on how she and Poincie's lives became associated with Reverend Heath's. She recalled the morning the Reverend had discovered the newborn baby on the rectory doorstep. If Gatha at a tender age hadn't been gang-raped behind the Cat and Fiddle by Morgan's pirates, her insides injured to the point of infertility, she would no doubt have had a child of her own. The child would have been named Poincie, short for poinciana, the majestic tree with spreading limbs and blossoms in resplendent red, looking like the entire tree was on fire.

When Reverend Heath asked for Gatha's help in naming the child she decided Poincie could be the name of this child. But maybe she would be better off anywhere but Port Royal. No place for a girl-child. Gatha knew that from experience. Mercifully for Gatha, after her rape she had been sent off to Westmoreland as a house slave on a sugar plantation where she learned domestic duties and generally made herself useful. She knew neither mother nor father, her earliest memories being that of a young girl brought up like a mascot child at a house of ill repute in Port Royal with multiple and transient women who cared for her with varying degrees of supervision. She was determined that Poincie have a more wholesome upbringing. Gatha, now took on the responsibilities of foster-mother and thus filled the aching emptiness of her maternal arms.

After getting Heath's permission to plant a tree in the backyard, Gatha secured a poinciana sapling at the market the next day. She had dug a hole and half-filled it with a layer of rich topsoil. She then unwrapped a blood-stained handkerchief that revealed the baby's severed navel string. This she placed in the hole and planted the sapling above it, pounding firm the soil around the base of the plant until it stood straight and tall. She watered the sapling generously. *Dis child know neider father nor mother, jus' like me, but she a child of dis here land. Her roots will grow thick and deep in de soil of her island.*

Then came the day when Poincie came screaming to Gatha, walking on the sides of her heels, with her legs apart, blood running down the inside of her thighs. She was fearful that some awful unknown disease had overtaken her.

"Is awright, Darlin,'" Gatha had said, calming the girl and sat her down and explained how this was a good sign. "Nothin' to be scared of. Yu jus' need to save the clean rags and cloths so dat when de time come you use them to soak up de blood till it stop. Den you bury the 'blood cloths' when you get a chance. Is so we all do. Nothin' strange Darlin'. You turnin' woman now!" And she hugged Poincie, reassuring her.

As the years passed, Poincie helped Aunt Gatha in the kitchen and accompanied her to the market sometimes. On one such trip the market vendors remarked to Gatha how Poincie was growing so nicely and was such a pretty brown-skinned young woman. Poincie accepted these compliments demurely, blushingly.

Gatha, on one of these occasions, noticed the notorious Mary Carleton, Port Royal's infamous whore, out shopping in the market. This was the Mary Carleton who, ever since she came from England on a boat had become the most popular prostitute in Port Royal. She had earned a reputation for seducing the most virtuous men, if such could be found in Port Royal, and seemed to always get her way and achieve her purpose once she set her mind to it. She was dressed like an English lady and had a servant with her, but everyone knew that she made a living lying down on the job. The men in the market, most of whom couldn't afford her, would say she was like a barbershop chair: no sooner than one man was out, another was in.

Mary Carleton drifted by looking at the vendors and bargaining like a local. Gatha noticed that she cast her eye on Poincie and a cold chill ran down her spine. She not goin' get dis child in her business, no way. Not if Gatha had anything to say about it, and would let Reverend Heath know if she ever tried to get Poincie into her whorehouse just because she so good looking. Her good looks could be a blessing or a curse. Gatha grabbed Poincie by the arm and made a premature exit. As they passed through the market entrance and Gatha glanced over her shoulder, Mary Carleton was still looking in their direction. After that day, Gatha resolved never to send Poincie to the market alone.

Weeks turned to months and months to years, and one day Reverend Heath sat Poincie and Gatha down and explained that Poincie needed to make her way in the world and though he loved her as a daughter and would miss her, he had arranged to have her hired as a house servant at Stokes Hall. It was a start, he said, though she was more than qualified to be a nanny. Later, when Kwaku came by with Calypso, Gatha noticed that Kwaku was crestfallen when she informed him that Poincie had relocated to the Stokes Hall Estate as a house servant. He sighed and said simply, "It look like dem might need some yam and banana over at Stokes Hall," and Gatha nodded and smiled.

CHAPTER FIVE

The Carleton Establishment

On his visits to Port Royal Kwaku followed his habit of visiting Gatha and Reverend Heath and then visiting the Carleton establishment. This way Gatha had the first choice of what he had to offer and the Maroons, who were growing uneasy, had current information garnered from his visits to Mary Carleton and elsewhere. Such produce as remained in Calypso's hampers he would sell in the marketplace or at residences he passed on his way there.

The Carleton place was Port Royal's most notorious whorehouse, but one could not sense its notoriety by judging merely from its appearance. It was a two-story structure with the typical green jalousie windows and the half timbers characterizing the English Tudor style. There was no sign to announce the true nature of the dwelling, but it would have been the pride of any upper-crust onlooker to call it home. Indeed it was, as far as the casual observer could tell, a retreat for the sophisticated, complete with a tavern and comfortable accommodations. One would see the arrival and departure of various men of means in their carriages driven by freedmen, colored mostly, although an indentured white man or two sometimes served as carriage drivers.

The house was set to the right of the plot of land on which it stood, conveniently leaving a side passage to its left where carriages could pass discreetly to the back yard of the property where livery attendants ensured the care of horses and where drivers commiserated as they waited to convey their drunken or satiated masters back to their respectable homes. Here, there was no chance a commodore would ever encounter a midshipman, nor a planter a backra. Here sundry men of means and women of easy virtue gathered in the evening hours.

When Kwaku reached this establishment on one of his visits, it was later in the day. The evening was balmy and overcast with the moon a mere glow behind a shroud of cloud spanning the entirety of the sky. He took the side entrance to the backyard where patrons would sometime gather under the back veranda. To Kwaku's left was a shed behind which a tall palm was silhouetted against the slate-grey sky. In front of the shed was a little rivulet of seawater which filled and emptied with the ebb and flow of the tide while a few yards from the beach lay moored a vessel, its crossbeams tilted and its sails draped neatly up and out of the breeze. To the right of the rivulet was where the action was.

A naked black slave was on a slightly raised wooden platform, winding and contorting her body in a sinuous way to the rhythms of a string instrument played by another. A dark-skinned drummer maintained a steady staccato in hypnotic rhythms. The music was barely audible under the raucous din of reckless laughter and intermittent shouts and outbursts of delight from male and female voices blended in a cacophony of celebration so unlike the atmosphere in the polite stiffness of English manor houses.

One step higher than the wooden platform was another level where, under the thatched overhang of the back verandah there was a long table, benched on each side at which sat the center of conversation and attention. A newly returned gentleman was holding court with three women lounging languorously around him dressed in pastel colored dresses, their bosoms bared to spare only their nipples. There were eager listeners, tankards in their hands, scattered around, some sitting on steps, others on wicker chairs, yet others on barrels once filled with rum. Their clothing shone in their satin blues, reds, browns and yellows from the glow of lanterns hanging from the supporting posts of the overhang and from one centrally placed on the table.

Above, from the second story, a latticed window had been thrown open and a prostitute was leaning out, watching the slave dancer and the mob below, laughing at the jokes coming from beneath the thatched overhang below her. Above her hung the three-quarter moon now veiled by wispy layers of cirrus cloud looking down as if in mild bemusement at the scene below. Tongues loosened by rum, spirits enlivened by tales of piracy and naval warfare, visions of plunder and booty danced through the heads of men and women, and even a few slaves and carriage drivers hovering subdued in the shadows seemed caught up in the celebratory mood. It was an energizing scene but one that Kwaku watched with curiosity rather than envy.

Miss Carleton's maid told him on his inquiry that the woman was "occupied" for the moment, so he asked for the conveyance of his regards until next morning. He returned next morning. She was not as busy and greeted him as an old acquaintance. While she inspected his ground provisions for purchase they chit-chatted. Though they were of different social classes in the Jamaican social hierarchy, they both shared common ground among the marginalized. There was also a good-naturedness and an endearing demeanor in

Kwaku that Mary Carleton recognized, in contrast to the clientele that patronized her establishment, so occasionally she felt comfortable in taking him into her confidence. This time she seemed to need all his remaining ground provisions, a lucky prospect, although Kwaku wondered what occasion would necessitate the stocking of extra food.

"Howdy Miss Carleton! How you doin' Ma'am?"

"Fine Kwaku. How are things up in the country?"

"Not too bad, Ma'am. But life hard and de grung tough."

"Life is hard for everybody, Kwaku."

"Business not good Ma'am?"

"No. It's just sometimes some of these people get on my nerves."

"Dese people?"

"Yes, some of these planters come and bed down me and the girls then look down at us and pass remarks when they are in their polite company. The wives think they are better than me because I get money for sleeping with men, including their husbands, when we all know that they also sleep with their husbands in return for their money and what they inherit when the men keel over."

"True wud Ma'am."

"And the planters themselves go to church every Sunday, all pious and holy, while they screw the negro women and have the negro slaves work the sugar cane. Don't they realize that they profit from human flesh just like me? They no better than me! As a matter of fact, I am better than them because I am giving pleasure while they profit from cruelty and pain. Now, you tell me Kwaku, which is better?"

"I see what yu mean Ma'am. Now, when is the next ship comin' in Ma'am?"

"They come in every day, but I hear that one from England is coming in day after tomorrow."

"Lots of booty ashore that day."

"Yes, Kwaku. Last week a soldier was here and he was drunk as a bat, couldn't rise to the occasion, if you know what I mean, but he was loose with his tongue and told me that an English vessel was due in a day or two and that the haul this time was good.

"Yes Ma'am. Good fe business."

The banter continued while Kwaku inwardly reflected that it was good to have Mary Carleton as one of his clients though he was not one of hers.

Kwaku lingered in Port Royal after his hampers had been almost emptied of ground provisions. The prospect of an arriving ship from England was particularly intriguing. What kind of cargo might it bring? It would be smart to linger long enough to find out. In the meanwhile, he would keep a low profile and monitor the scene. He tethered Calypso to a post in the open-air marketplace, spread a rough straw mat under the donkey and lay there, sheltered from the sun by the faithful beast as it chewed on provisions he had brought from the hills.

He appeared to be asleep, but every rumor and nearby conversation became the object of his awareness as he watched the movement of vessels, goods, and people through half-closed eyes. Nearby, two pirates leaned against a shed in their pantaloons, brown vests and loose shirts, their heads topped with tri-cornered hats as they smoked their chalk pipes, puffing through the corner of their mouths as they talked. They were obviously drunk. Other higglers and tradesmen carried on a lively banter as they sold their wares.

One popular topic of conversation was the discovery of the body of Backra Swaby, a Justice of the Peace no less, near the cotton tree on the Spanish Town road. The man had been battered in the head. There was speculation as to who would do such a thing, but some locals were convinced that duppies had finally given Backra his due. After all, slave duppies were known to dwell in the roots and branches of the tree and when they had a chance to kill the backra, they took it. What other explanation could there be? So now there would be a white duppy and many black duppies from the slaves hanged there. Would the slave duppies take revenge on the white duppy? Can duppy kill duppy? Some locals wanted to know.

Some in the market, including mulattoes and white women, said that there was a rumor about a bookkeeper named Bolt who went missing and that the authorities thought there might be some connection between the two events, Bolt, like the dead backra, having left the Ferry Inn the morning of Justice Swaby's death. In any case, Bolt, if he were found and alive, would be apprehended forthwith for questioning.

Kwaku thought of how lucky he had been so far. That incident at the cotton tree had changed his life in far-reaching ways. Unexpected events can so radically change the course of one's life. Those first few days as a fugitive were very disturbing. Fleeing to the hills, trudging on through the bushes farther and farther into the interior, almost dying of thirst was not a pleasant experience to one who had not been hardened by torturous work in the cane fields. Clothes were ripped by sharp rocks and thorns seemed to grasp at clothing on the way through thick underbrush. Eventually, the welcoming waters of the Stony River appeared. That was a good place to camp and to think. He was not quite sure what could be done for the long term, but one must be determined to cope with the short term until circumstances indicated the next best move. It was best to stay close to the Stony River and built a lean-to.

First, he created a large square frame of poles enclosing a gridwork of smaller sticks thus fashioning a panel of interwoven vines covered with large leaves, all tied together with small vines. Then he used two poles to prop up the panel with one side still resting on the ground. This crude partition could move around from one direction to another to shelter from the wind or rain. This lean-to needed one more feature: a hammock on which to sleep. Vines were adequate to fashion a long interwoven basket-like accommodation with one end secured to a tree and the other to a rocky outcropping. He would live like a Taino for the foreseeable future. The Tainos originally used Port Royal as a fishing camp before the white man dispossessed them of that land. This was, after all, part of the island legacy.

He bathed in the river and went foraging for wild fruits and berries. He made a slingshot from the elastic that held the gatherings at the foot of leggings but with no fire there was no point of shooting the birds that were abundant in the woods. He went barefoot occasionally to allow the calluses on the feet to develop. It was painful at first, but that was the price for freedom.

Then one morning came some scantily clad Negroes, three in all, who seemed to be passing through. At first they were as startled to see him as he was to see them, but eventually they were convinced that he was alone and meant no harm. He offered them his coat, and most of the change of clothing that he had brought with him. They in return gave flint and matches, a gourd, a machete, and some ground provisions. They were Maroons from farther up in the hills. Some of the ground provisions were saved to start a field to grow sweet potatoes, yams, cocoa, dasheens, and a few herbs and spices the Maroons had brought. Later, the hammock was lined with rough crocus bags and old clothing secured from the Maroons.

Soon they trusted enough to share with him somewhat of their way of life and although they had never disclosed their encampment, wherever that was, an affinity for them developed and their way of life seemed so wholesome. They agreed to never mention his whereabouts to anyone outside of their circle. A simple way of life evolved by selling ground provisions as the cultivation expanded and additional ground provisions could be secured from the Maroons who came down occasionally from above the escarpment that was visible in the far distance from the Stony River.

Years went by and use of the King's English was abandoned in favor of the local patois learned at his mother's knees. He could not dare revert to his persona as John Bolt. The beard was by now mature, complexion deepened by the sun, and the torso was rippling with well-defined muscles. Selling goods in the markets, he finally ventured into Port Royal itself, and became a regular vendor known as Kwaku.

After a while his frugality paid off, and he was able to buy a donkey in the market and named him Calypso, a name he had overheard in his rounds at the homes where he now stopped to sell his wares. He liked the name Calypso. It had a musical ring and rhythm to it. His hands had acquired the necessary hardness and calluses characteristic of small farmers and he held them with some pride. It was so good to be close to the earth and to enjoy its goodness, even if he had to forego the level of amenities to which he had become accustomed. Female companionship was the only thing lacking in his life. It wasn't long before his Maroon compatriots asked him to be their eyes and ears in that important enclave of power brokers and commerce that was Port Royal. Bolt had become Kwaku, and Kwaku had become a spy.

As it turned out, a fair wind had brought the expected vessel sooner than anticipated. Kwaku watched it gingerly approach the dock and its moorings. From the water level on its side he could tell that the vessel was heavily laden and the number of heads peering toward the shore meant that both people and goods made for a heavy payload. When the ramps were lowered, the disembarking passengers could be seen to represent a cross-section of British society, returnees having the assured demeanor of the seasoned traveller, while first-time arrivals looked on with the uneasy curiosity of a dog encountering a snake in its path.

Next came the cargo. There were the usual trunks with personal effects, crates of imported goods to stock the shelves of shops and apparel stores, furniture from the homeland, boxes with choice preserved meats, canned and packaged products of all kinds, building materials including bricks, and haberdashery of various descriptions. These were carted away after officials of the customs house nearby had satisfied themselves in due deliberative fashion that the proper tariff or excise had been properly exacted and that King Charles was all the richer for the arrival of the vessel, albeit from England. This was no slave ship so Kwaku was spared the displeasure of witnessing a slave auction. The poor brutes would have been finally exhumed from the bowels of the vessel and paraded as so many cattle on the auction platform that bore a striking resemblance to a gallows on which some runaways would sometimes swing in the wind.

Presently he noticed members of the local militia and red-jacketed soldiers clustering around an array of large boxes fitted with several handles as one would see on a coffin for the convenience of pallbearers, except that these boxes were clearly larger than coffins. Kwaku noticed that they were covered with tarpaulins with cut-outs to allow the handles to protrude while concealing the box itself. These were loaded onto multiple carts driven by soldiers and headed toward the government buildings and the general vicinity of the governor's mansion.

Kwaku followed discreetly, walking his donkey as if to sell his wares but never losing sight of the laden carts ahead of him. So what if they contained arms and ammunition? They were too heavily guarded to be stolen. Everyone knew that the forts were well manned, and the armory was particularly well guarded. Baited on, Kwaku followed behind at a safe distance.

Presently, one cart laden with two containers diverged from the group and took the gravel road leading out of Port Royal. The driver was a young backra and with him were four others, two soldiers and two local militiamen, judging from their modes of dress. He recognized the young backra as Jack Hart. Poincie, now a grown young woman, had told him about Massa Jack on one of his visits to the Stokes Hall estate. He recognized him from one of his earlier visits there. So the arms were going to Stokes Hall.

Kwaku mounted his donkey and headed for the hills. The first impulse was to follow the cart to Stokes Hall and bring Poincie into his confidence but he thought the better of it and decided to consult with his Maroon contacts first. This was not a one-man job and too much was at stake.

CHAPTER SIX

Theodicy and Idiocy

Lewis Galdy closed the barbershop and with his bag of instruments made his way towards the rectory of Reverend Emmanuel Heath. The cobblestone alleys of Port Royal were always pungent with the smell of rum that, once one got accustomed to it, was then wafted away by the sea breeze, and then a fresh reminder of the debauchery came with the next wave of alcoholic stench. Galdy waved his decline of an invitation from an inebriate and his two minions as they invited him to join them on the steps outside a tavern. They were taking turns at swigging from a small cask of rum purchased by one of them. Their slurred speech meant they would not remember to be offended by his refusal and would still patronize his shop when they sobered up enough to see their need for a haircut.

As a poor white, he felt privileged to be summoned to trim the reverend's hair at the private residence of the Anglican clergyman and especially so because it was a two-fold advantage: the reverend made it worth his while to close the barber shop to the local clientele and since Lewis was an occasional back-seat attendee at St. Paul's, he liked exchanging ideas with the reverend. An audience with a man of Heath's stature would not have been afforded him under any other circumstance.

With a freshly laundered sheet draped around the clergyman and pinned behind his neck, Lewis prepared to shave and trim Heath's overgrown gunmetal hair. The swivel chair in the study served as the barber's chair.

"What brought you to this island, Lewis?"

"*T'sais*, tis a long story, Reverend."

"I am all ears, Lewis."

"Well, I was born in Montpelier, France in 1659. My family was Protestant Hugenot and Louis XIV was determined to convert us to Catholicism by any means possible. He used missionaries, punishments, and force to convert us, and declared our religion illegal. We were also forbidden to leave the country, but many of us fled to many other places in Europe and Africa. My brother Laurent and I and a few thousand others ended up here in the British colonies, also in New York and South Carolina. That is how Laurent and I ended up in Port Royal."

"I see. I am glad you found a church home at St. Paul's."

"*Quais, enfin*, I am not a regular attender, Reverend, but tis good to know the church is there if I ever feel a need."

"Good to see you in church last Sunday, Lewis."

"Always a pleasure Reverend."

"Feel free to sit closer to the front next time."

"Aye, Reverend. If I don't arrive late."

"So, what did you think of the sermon?"

"You mean Sodom and Gomorrah? Well, 'twas a fitting message to the ne'er-do-wells of Port Royal Reverend...."

"But you hesitate. What else is on your mind?"

"The church people took it well, but 'tis like preaching to the converted, Reverend."

"Point well taken. With one tavern for every eighty people on Port Royal how can I pull people away from the bottle long enough to get a message across to them?"

"Almos' impossible. Rogues, whores and rum: That's the sum of Port Royal. Much like Sodom and Gomorrah. Some say we will end up like them."

" I certainly hope not, my friend. But sometimes I feel like Jonah preaching to Nineveh, except these people don't readily turn from their ways."

" But you must admit Reverend that after a night of riotous living, many come repentant to church next Sunday mornin'."

"This is true, I grant you, but only a few who feel some guilt. It is like penance for them."

"Yes sir, but in my shop last week one of the fellas said those blokes in Sodom and Gomorrah were damned (pardon Reverend) fools for building two cities near a volcano. They were asking for a disaster. Anodder fella said Port Royal was no better. He was a stonemason and no house in Port Royal has any real foundation because not two feet down they hit the water table. We are built on a sandbar. So many people in such a small space and not much to hold it all up. He told the odder fellow that we 'ave our own problems and Sodom had theirs. The Spaniards built wooden houses but the English built with lots of stone on the sand."

"Not very smart of us."

"Aye Reverend. *C'est nul.* Didn't the good Lord talk about wise and foolish builders, those on the rock and the foolish on the sand?"

"Hmm. I can feel a sermon coming on, Lewis."

By this time Lewis' razor was expertly scanning the vulnerable expanse of the pious throat and his sudden reticence became understandable. Lewis no longer pressed the issue. There were so many questions he would have liked to press on the good reverend. If God is all-powerful and all-loving how come he seems to ignore the cries of those He loves? Why did He kill the innocent children of Sodom and Gomorrah? And the innocent children and adults who seem to suffer the same fate as the wicked? Why didn't God protect Abel who "pleased God" while Cain, the first murderer, He protected with a special mark? How can God feel our immediate pain if He has complete foreknowledge, and if He feels our pain, how come He seems so cowardly, feeling much but doing nothing? What comfort is the belief that He feels our pain if He chooses to merely sit and watch and suffer with us? Does He care about the slaves being oppressed, even massacred, by the evil triangular trade that enriches these people of Europe? Either this god is all-loving but not all-powerful, or he is all-powerful but not all-loving. That seemed certain to Lewis Galdy.

The shaving complete, Galdy turned to the task of trimming the Reverend's hair. He ventured upon another less controversial subject.

"Reverend, you mention Jonah and just a fortnight ago I was reading the story about Jonah and the whale."

"Yes, That is one of my favorite stories in the Good Book."

"Mine too, sir, but some things were a bit puzzling to me."

"Go on."

"Well, after I read it for meself for the first time in the Good Book, the story seems to have so many, shall we say, details which stretch the truth, almost like a fairy tale. Well, *laisser tomber.*"

"Go on."

"The whole idea of an eight-word sermon offering nary any hope, but converting every single wicked person in the big heathen city of Nineveh; the scene of hogs, sheep, cattle, and horses all dressed up in sackcloth and covered in ashes all repenting along with the people. Pardon Reverend but this looks ridiculous."

Reverend Heath chuckles, and sensing no remonstrance from the clergyman, Galdy continued.

"The idea that a vine can spring up to full height and die down all within a day; that Jonah could live in a fish for three days and when vomited up he was fully recovered and went on to preach....Reverend, that sounds, pardon Reverend, almost ludricous!"

"Well, indeed it is Lewis, but you miss the point. These stories were never intended to be taken literally. A story does not have to be true to illustrate a truth. The story of Jonah, the serpent in the Garden of Eden, many of the miracle stories, these were all intended to teach very important lessons. If we get distracted by the miraculous in these stories, then we miss the point the stories were intended to teach. For example, the

Jonah story was about rebirth, a new beginning."

"I did suspect that idea Reverend; it's just that I couldn't stop thinking of the big fish and poor ole Jonah inside. He must have given the fish a bad case of the stomach gripe."

They both chuckle as Lewis finished his task. He resolved to bother the Reverend no more on this particular subject, but was grateful for his candor and felt a special bond with the clergyman. Not many churchmen would engage a layperson in a discussion of this sort.

" You see, Lewis, the Israelites sometimes spoke of their history in metaphors and then we made the metaphors into history."

"So, Reverend, if these stories are not altogether true and the parishioners hear about that, won't some of them get disgusted and stop coming to church on Sunday morning?"

"Perhaps. People can choose to believe what they want. But church is not all about beliefs and faith. Church is about having some place to go when you have nowhere else. It provides support and hope in time of need. It serves a useful purpose regardless of the beliefs. I am a servant of the people at all stages of their life Church is where you go for christening, marriage, and funerals.

" For hatch, match, and dispatch. Haha! I see. Thanks, Reverend."

Galdy fished a liquid dispenser from his bag, the tin kind with a broad circular base and a long spout, and with his thumb pressed the base to release the liquid onto the reverend's head through the spout, working the sweet-smelling liquid into the neatly trimmed hair. "That isn't a hair-grower now, Lewis, is it?"

"No Reverend. Just something to freshen up the scalp," Galdy responded with a chuckle. Galdy held up the portable hand mirror for the clergyman's scrutiny of his face, shifted it to each side, and referred him to the large mirror on the wall behind them as he afforded the reverend a view of the back of his head. Satisfied, Heath handed him a handsome recompense and thanked him for his service.

CHAPTER SEVEN

The Young Backra

Jack Hart was fresh from his trip to Port Royal, having safely brought to Stokes Hall the two large boxes entrusted to his care. These he delivered to George Bradford and they both placed them in the lower room of the great house where was stashed also a generous supply of rum, liqueurs, and various exotic spirits. He returned to his own modest cottage to what sounded like drumming inside the house. What in heavens was going on?

As he entered the front door, he saw the drummer: a young servant he had inquired about earlier that week. She was on all fours, her back toward him, her short but ragged skirt sufficiently elevated to afford a generous view of the back of her legs and thighs as she worked feverishly, polishing the wooden floor with a coconut brush. As she worked, she maintained a steady rhythm with the brush as she polished each plank in the floor, the back hem of her skirt waving to and fro from her backside as she recited a chant to the rhythm of her brush strokes:

"Mosquito one,
Mosquito two.
Mosquito jump inna hot callaloo!"

Jack hesitated before alerting her to his presence. Besides, she seemed to be actually enjoying her task, even as he took some pleasure in observing her do it. Presently, his shadow became evident on the gleaming floor, a stark contrast to the unpolished portion that she doggedly assaulted with her rhythms.

"Pard'n Massa. Backra sen me to clean yu floor sence it neva clean so long now, sar. Careful how you walk Massa. It slippery and can mek yu slip an fall on yu backside, sar." A sliver of a smile escaped the side of her mouth.

Poincie had turned to face him, sitting back on her legs tucked under her, her generous bottom resting on her upturned heels, but not before she gathered her skirt and tucked it neatly into her crotch in a show of modesty, seemingly unaware that her action left yet visible a broad expanse of thigh. She was a "brown skin gal" with her hair caught up and away from her face, the full volume of it sheathed by a scarf tied at the base of her head. She held up her chin as she spoke to him and never once looked him in the eye, but as she turned her head aside the faint impression of a dimpled chin became visible.

She had higher than usual cheekbones and a smooth golden-brown honeyed complexion, which attributes made it obvious to Jack that she was a half-breed. Maybe a child of one of the prostitutes from Port Royal? A bastard child of a planter from a neighboring estate? A pirate's daughter? Her manner of dress and her general demeanor showed that she was no house slave, but a free woman who despite her demeaning status in life was a person in whom there was more depth of character and more cultural awareness than was obvious to the casual observer.

"What do they call you?"

"My name is Poinciana, but dey call me Poincie."

Hmmm...the Poinciana tree. Spreading limbs and fiery blossoms...

"Aren't you a servant in Backra's house? "

"Yes, Massa, but him say you need help cleanin' and such. Me could 'elp yu Massa. Backra say once a week me to come here."

"Is that all Backra said you should help me with?"

"Yes, Massa. But if yu 'ave anyting else..."

"That will be sufficient. Thank you. Carry on."

Earlier, Jack had seen the young mulatto and asked what she did on the estate. The Backra had volunteered that she cooked, cleaned, washed clothes and generally made herself useful. He would need such a servant occasionally to keep his lodgings in good shape. "But watch out for that one," Backra cautioned. "She was raised by Parson Heath and is like a daughter to him. Every time he comes here he asks for her. He and Lord Stokes are close friends. Any messing with her would get back to Stokes. Trust me, you don't want that."

Jack knew that a brown-skinned girl like her would become either a prostitute or a house worker, not much better than a slave. For most brown-skinned girls being a prostitute or a house servant would some times be indistinguishable. However, Backra had not taken advantage of her in that way. Perhaps it was because Backra would not want to incur the wrath of the big Massa by having Heath turn against him for any indiscretion he may commit. After all, Backra had the run of all the servants and slave women at his disposal. Still, Poinciana, like forbidden fruit, held a certain allure.

Jack observed that the males on Stokes Hall Estate could somewhat avoid the backra by cooperating, doing what they were supposed to, avoiding trouble. The women, however, had no such luxury. They were to be producers, reproducers, the object of white seducers, of whom Backra was the chief. Only the very young or the very old were spared his sexual impositions. He was known to visit Port Royal on a Saturday or Sunday for the sole purpose of screwing the Spanish and white prostitutes, merely as a diversion from the mostly Negro fare he enjoyed during the week. On those occasions Bradford left Jack Hart in charge of the estate until his return.

On other occasions he was known to ride over to the Slave Row at night leaving his missis at the house on the knoll located just below the Great House, and summon a woman of his choice from the family hut. She would follow him on foot to the cane piece and he would, as best he could, for he was reputed to be deficient in manly hardware, impose his will on her. Other times he would back a house servant behind a staircase in the large pantry of the Great House when the big Massa was away and let her handle his sweaty way to satiation.

All this Jack gleaned from listening to the patois which he was able to partially comprehend after months of exposure to the talk of the house slaves as well as those in the fields. Occasionally, Bradford would throw the hapless victim two bits as a token of his satisfaction. His dissatisfaction, however, was fraught with peril because failure to please Backra could mean reassignment to the arduous work of the fields and severe whippings for imagined shortcomings. The women knew that groaning and heavy breathing were recommended with Backra, but giggling was a sure–fire way to get sent to the fields as a manual laborer, even if the woman was already visibly pregnant.

Jack was grateful that he had not, as he initially hoped, been assigned to one of the twenty two estates in Westmoreland owned by the Beckfords because it was well known that William Beckford preferred men, especially those of European vintage. But Poincie, she was a welcome sight that occasionally graced his humble cottage. He looked forward to interacting with her. He would grasp every opportunity to get to know her despite Bradford's cautionary exhortation. It was his only ray of sunshine in an otherwise mundane and unsavory existence.

After Poincie finished her task, he thanked her, lay on his bed smelling the fresh polish applied to the floors and rested, his mind reflecting on how he came to be in this present situation. It was not long ago that he arrived and had first surveyed the simple lodgings that would be his home for the next several years. The bedroom was sparsely furnished with a plain wardrobe in one corner, an iron bed and a small table that held a washbasin, a goblet of water, and a wooden soap dish with a bar of soap. A small hand towel hung from a hook on the side. A faded etching of King Charles hung from the wall opposite the bed. Underneath the bed was a chipped porcelain chamber pot, called a "chimmy" for short, provided for nocturnal convenience. A kerosene oil lamp stood on the side of a small table with a chair.

The bed itself was one of those iron contraptions that looked like a torture rack with prison bars for a bedhead complete with floral knots that had long ago lost most of their porcelain. The bed was covered with a worn-out deep-pile bedspread, the kind that leaves a pattern on one's face if one chose to sleep on it. The glass shade on the lamp beside the bed had the inscription Home Sweet Home. Home sweet home, indeed.

England and childhood seemed so far away now. Five thousand miles across an ocean. An immense distance. But what was one supposed to do? There was no way a young man could make a decent living in his local English village. His own father had said it so many times that finally Jack saw the inevitability of his leaving to seek his fortune elsewhere. The family was of modest means, and the English doctrine called The Law of Primogeniture dictated that upon the death of the father the first son would inherit the father's estate, leaving nothing to the second son. The latter was then at the mercy of the older brother and whatever level of generosity he was inclined to extend to the younger sibling. Jack was not particularly close to his older brother and the estate was a modest one. He cursed the fate that relegated him to this unfortunate circumstance.

There was little comfort in his father's Anglican religion. The sermons from the local vicar on a Sunday morning only added to his misery and hopelessness. Almost all the Bible stories seemed to show that the younger son was the preferred son. Abel and Cain, Jacob and Esau, Isaac and Ishmael, Joseph and his brothers: the younger always gained preference over the older sons. Why was it not that way now in Christian England? Instead, there were limited options: the military or the priesthood, neither of which held any appeal for Jack Hart.

Everyone knew that sugar and slavery in the West Indies were the only way for someone such as he to make his mark and become anything approaching wealthy. The vast British Empire needed men to maintain its hold on the locals and administer the affairs of the colonies. There was a shortage of white overseers, accountants, and artisans on many sugar plantations in Jamaica. He had no qualifications in those areas but he was assured that his white skin was more than enough. He would be trained on the job. When the opportunity presented itself he jumped at it.

Shortly after his arrival, the overseer George Bradford had introduced Jack to his new arena and responsibilities as an assistant overseer. Backra Bradford was a short, pudgy, hairy-chested man, red-skinned from long exposure to the sun. Leathery wrinkles covered his neck, his bulbous cheeks shaded by a wide brimmed straw hat and his eyes habitually squinted against the assault of the fierce Caribbean sun. His double chin revealed a deep dimple that stubbornly resisted the encroachment of surrounding tissue. He was constantly sweating and carried a dirty kerchief of questionable hue tied around his neck for the sole purpose of wiping his face.

Bradford carried a horsewhip tucked in his waistband. This was the whip he soaked every night in a basin of lime juice to add extra sting to the lashes he inflicted on the backs of the field hands. On the opposite side of his barrel of a belly, were two pistols tucked under his thick belt. His large cast-iron belt buckle was precariously perched on the apex of his paunch and threatened to slip below at a moment's notice. He spoke as he paced to and fro, with authoritarian waddle, giving Jack initial instructions.

He introduced Jack to branding irons and the open half-stove in which hot coals blazed to ensure a more than skin-deep branding of each slave. He showed him the hammers used for pounding slowly and incessantly on the fingernails of subjects under interrogation until a confession was extracted or that was used to punish recaptured runaways. Jack had noticed that some slaves' hands showed numerous fused finger joints.

Then there were the wooden clappers that could be screwed tighter and tighter to crush the genitals of males. There were, of course, the tamarind switch and the deadly cat-o-nine tails, each tipped with glass or metal shards to rip open the skin of a rebellious slave. Bradford displayed these with the pride of a doctor demonstrating the newest surgical instruments.

"There is a large wooded area at the back of the estate where you need to keep an eye because that is a likely spot for niggas to escape, and there is a river running through it. You need to see this area for yourself and be familiar with it. If the returns are good, after the harvest we hope to clear that land and put in sugar cane to increase our exports of sugar and rum. Be armed when you go and better in the daytime. More than one white man has disappeared into that wood never to return alive."

CHAPTER EIGHT

Runaways?

It was four in the morning at the slave village of the Stokes Hall Estate. Shadowy figures stirred in the chill of the morning air, while emaciated dogs yelped at no one in particular, just to assure themselves that they could still make their presence known. The rough outlines of the slave barracks could barely be seen in the morning mist and the wattle-and-mud huts built by the slaves to accommodate their growing numbers could be detected between and behind the barracks, near to the little plots of rugged land which slaves were allowed to cultivate. These plots were used to supplement the diet of the slaves and also to build their savings toward someday buying their freedom as they sold ground provisions.

Cudjoe had come awake earlier in his slave hut and, bones aching from over-exertion. He had remained immobile on the thin burlap crocus bag filled with leaves which served as his bed. Some slaves used the shredded coconut husks, called "kaya" to fill these bags to form a crude mattress. Cudjoe thought of the soul-searing Middle Passage and the survival of Little Nanny, now nine years old, and a few others he had come to know.

He remembered the Anancy stories he had heard as a child in Africa, stories his enslaved brothers and sisters had carried with them to the New World. Anancy, a spider, was a humble and lowly creature in the general scheme of things but always managed to use his brains to gain the upper hand. He used "smarts" to neutralize the overwhelming odds stacked against him. There was a principle in those stories that could be applied to their situation, a strategy that must be found.

Some slaves had escaped to the hills to join those who had never bended their knees to the English. There is strength in unity and he, Johnny, Accompong, and Little Nanny would one day join forces with these Maroons. The planters had mixed Cudjoe's enslaved brothers and sisters from different tribes so that language differences would reduce the risk of conspiracy to revolt. Initially his siblings had separated themselves so that their association went undetected. They were fortunate to be still together. What the planters didn't know was that the various languages were being merged into a common patois that made communication possible between different African tribes on the plantation. Patois was the glue that held together the community of the enslaved.

First, they must escape from this place. That was a prospect fraught with extreme danger. He knew only too well the punishment meted out to runaways. He must block from his mind the spectacle of the degradation meted out to those unfortunates. It wouldn't do to dwell too long on that scene, except to plan the escape all the more meticulously to avoid such an outcome. The hills were calling, arousing a primeval longing for freedom and self-determination. The Middle Passage was hell enough and plantation life was another daily hell. This life was worse than death. The nearest thing to home was those hills and there is where they must go.

The backra said one day Cudjoe would make a good driver, a slave promoted to the position of driving the others with a whip to make them work harder, grow more cane to make Massa richer. How could he do that? The driver would be the one to kick and whip the women and men in the fields. When they got whipped at the stake with the cat-o-nine tipped with glass, the driver was the one who rubbed the salt and pepper into the wounds to make the punishment worse. And when the backra wanted to show that he was in charge, he took the driver's woman and screwed her as he liked, just to show who was boss.

In Africa, the traders used other Africans to catch others from other tribes to sell to the slave ships. Here in Jamaica one could see the stupidity of allowing the Europeans to use Africans of different tribes against their own people. No, he would never be a driver. He would have no part of it. Yet to defy the promotion was to court death. Instead, he must escape, but how?

Cudjoe must be careful, think this thing through. The best time would be at night after the last roll call and under the protection of darkness. The cane would add additional cover, but the north field would be harvested in the next two weeks and that cover would be gone. This couldn't wait much longer. Yet, they must hasten deliberately. Timing was everything. The night patrols. It would be a challenge to get around them. Must be a way to reduce that risk. If Cudjoe could find out who would be patrolling and when. And it was known that Backra Bradford occasionally took a weekend trip to Port Royal leaving Massa Jack to keep an eye on things. The girl Poincie seemed close to Massa Jack, cooking and cleaning for him and running jokes with him sometimes. If he could get close enough to her....

Cudjoe remembered the time when he was bringing the cane on his back to the sugar mill. He, bent over, looked sideways under his load as he sensed he was being stared at. It was the young backra. He averted his eyes, but not before he received an almost imperceptible nod of acknowledgement from the young massa. Cudjoe did not know what this meant, if anything, but did not respond in case he suffered a negative consequence. There was no knowing what was going through a backra's mind. Holding a massa's gaze too long was deemed insolence, punishable by extreme beatings and torture.

The daily routine on the plantation left very little opportunity for escape. It was approaching the fifth hour and the clang-clang of the clarion said it was time for Cudjoe to get moving. The animals had to be fed, the machetes to be counted and distributed, and the slaves to attack the cane fields. Cudjoe grabbed some dirty rice from a gourd and stuffed it in his mouth. He could not be late for the roll call or he would be punished severely. Just last week Backra had a slave wear a neck ring to which additional weights were attached to increase the burden and which did not allow a person to sit until released from the contraption. Cudjoe more than once had felt the sharp sting of the driver's whip when the driver decided that his movement in the early morning was too lethargic. It was known that when Backra came near the drivers would whip with enthusiasm, but when alone the drivers would crack the whip near the skin of those they favored, sometimes without making contact.

The stalks of the sugarcane, some up to twelve feet tall, were slashed at the root, the tall leaves cut off and the cane dropped on the ground to be picked up by others following behind. At the end of the day these would be carried and carted off to the sugar mill. Blades rose and fell, glistening in the early morning light and whips snapped an unpredictable staccato. Soon the bodies of Negroes exuded rivers of sweat and the sunlight danced over bare backs and rippling muscles.

It was the eighth hour, time for breakfast. Cudjoe and the others wended their way from the cane fields to the canteen, a long grass-covered hut with rough-hewn boards for a table and similar slats for benches along the extended table. He eagerly swallowed mouthfuls of boiled yams, eddoes, and okra seasoned with peppers and salt. Late-comers to the canteen would be whipped and sometimes deprived of nourishment for the day. Again, any absences were readily detected.

The work of the day resumed and went on until noon. It was a very tiring time under the fierce blaze of the sun. Some slaves were grateful that at breakfast they had drunk the pot water used to boil the yams and eddoes. Water was in short supply and was distributed only during the breaks. Cudjoe mechanically cut the cane, his muscles from long arduous practice conditioned to do the work correctly while his mind studied every detail of his surroundings and daily routine. His body was in the field but his mind was on more desperate musings. From midday till the second hour he returned to the canteen for a meal and the slave quarters for a much-needed rest.

He had to return for yet another roll call at the third hour when the clang-clang of the bell aroused him. This would be the most difficult part of his day. He would have to work till the sixth hour of the evening. So far Cudjoe had had no flash of insight, no ingenious plan for escape. So far, the routine did not allow for any leeway, compounded by the fact that he must take with him Little Nanny, Accompong, and Johnny. He must not leave them behind. Besides, if he escaped solo then they may suffer the brunt of Backra's wrath.

The day wore on, and fatigue began to take its toll. By now the canes were being carried to the sugar mill on oxcarts and the backs of the workers. Cudjoe neared the mill like a beast of burden with stalks of cane tied together and placed on his back. He walked with mincing steps, bent over to balance the load when, glancing around, he saw the spectacle of a Negro walking the treadmill outside the large barn housing the sugar mill. This beast had slackened his pace and this had not gone unnoticed. He was walking the treadmill, desperately hanging onto a crossbar with a taut rope around his neck, the other end tied to an overhanging tree. Any slackening of his pace and he would hang.

The acquisition of this device was one in which Backra Bradford had taken an inordinate pride. Newly invented in Leiden, Holland, it consisted of a large wooden cylindrical paddlewheel fitted with ridges and called "the eternal staircase" which one or sometimes two slaves were required to climb, producing the energy to pump water and in some cases grind grain, hence the change from the original name "treadwheel" to "treadmill." It was a torture device deriving its terror from the sheer monotony that Backra Bradford further intensified with the imminent potential for hanging.

The treadmill would cease turning by nightfall. Both Bradford and Hart had seemingly forgotten about the slave. He was getting old anyway. One less mouth to feed.

At the sixth hour Cudjoe returned to his hut in Slaves Row. Bread and rancid butter was his supper, washed down with sugar-and-water.

The sugarcane harvest was in full swing. This meant longer working hours, more harsh punishments for imagined "slackness" and more desperate whippings from the drivers who themselves were under threat of demotion, floggings, or sale to another plantation. There, their reputation for brutality to their own would have meant sure recrimination from fellow slaves who exacted extreme penalty, their vitriol heaped upon the driver as the closest surrogate to the backra or the absentee master.

The center of this frenzied activity was the sugar mill, operated in sustained momentum twenty-four hours a day for weeks. The mill was housed in a large barn-like structure with dirt floors. The cane was brought in by cart after cart drawn by oxen or donkeys, and in a steady stream the canes were fed into large stone or metallic rollers that squeezed and extracted the cane juice that then was channeled into large vats. Those rollers were driven by a steam engine fed by a constant supply of wood. The driver was always cracking his whip and urging the wood gatherers and cane transporters to keep up a frantic pace, each dependent on the other for the steady production of cane juice which was then refined into sugar. The fire under the vats was constantly fed by logs supplied by several slaves who also stirred the cane juice with long poles like paddles.

The smell was sickeningly sweet and pungent, mixed with the sweaty odor of naked bodies glistening and mingling with the flashes of flickering flames and steam, an assault on the senses. The sugar produced was contained in hogsheads loaded onto carts and transported to the docks where they would be shipped to sweeten the plum puddings, scones, and teas of the European aristocracy.

In the still-house nearby was the other major center of activity where the refined and fermented liquid was transformed into the potent rum which was then poured into puncheons and also transported to the nearest port and sent off to lighten the spirits and pockets of rich Europeans, mainly Englishmen.

All hands were busy; all bodies were in a state of perpetual motion and a buzz of activity typical of any factory. All that is, except one: a tall jet-black slave, motionless, standing with arms folded, as if at attention, the flickering flames spasmodically illuminating his glistening smooth black skin, as he stood in statuesque dignity. Cudjoe always admired the tall, regal bearing of his younger brother, Johnny. He was holding an axe which itself shone with the play of the flickering light on its sharpened edge. Johnny seemed fixated on the rollers and the cane fed into them. He seemed hypnotized by the mechanics of the crushing machine.

The movements of the slaves became more and more robot-like as the fatigue of sixteen-hour days and nights seemed to create automatic movement and numbness to pain and tiredness as they fed the machines with the long stalks of sugarcane. Eventually, the humanity of the poor wretches took over and the result of extreme fatigue took its toll: there was a yelp loud enough to be heard above the din of activity. A slave feeding the canes into the rollers had not withdrawn his hand quickly enough and was being drawn inexorably into the crushing stone rollers, his fingers and then his hand crushed, bones flattened, as he yelled in pain.

Immediately Johnny leaped into action with the alertness and ferocity of a jaguar. There was a flash of steel as down came the axe onto the forearm of the poor brute feeding the cane in to the rollers. The man collapsed onto the ground grabbing what was left of his right arm as blood spurted from the stump left after his forearm, now on its way to the vats, was severed just below the elbow.

Johnny had temporarily saved the man's life by chopping off his arm. He grabbed his own cloth belt and made a tourniquet that he applied to the stump whereupon two other slaves carried off the maimed man. He would die by morning. Another slave rescued the mangled and flattened arm before it reached the vats, while blood mingled with sugarcane juice sluiced into the channel. The momentum of the work continued with barely a break as relentlessly the driver pressed the task. Another Negro took the place of the victim and the axe-wielder resumed his statuesque posture. The mill continued its oppressive, monotonous grind into the night. Cudjoe noticed as a certain Reverend Heath, who was visiting the estate, quickly turned away into the darkness as his dark robes blended into the blackness of the night.

CHAPTER NINE

A Plan

Kwaku was always happy to see Poincie on his trips to the Stokes Hall Estate in the parish of St. Thomas. He would be the lone figure in green, and Calypso his donkey, coming up the long gravel road that led to the great house. Poincie recognized his gait and posture long before she could see his face clearly. Kwaku walked with a certain dignity that proclaimed his freedman status. This time she met him part way and they embraced as he neared Backra's house and sat under a mango tree as they commiserated.

"So how yu doin' Putoos?"

"Not so bad! How is Aunt Gatha?"

"Me see her one fortnight ago. Except for the arthritis and a likkle gas now and den, she doin all right."

"Good. Me miss her so till! Last week when Reverend Heath come here him did say him will ask Backra fi let me go look for her. Him come here once in a while to check up on tings for Lord Stokes, him and the lawyer who oversee the property. Backra extra hard on us when dem come visit, but still me glad because Reverend Heath always ask fe me and check pon me too. So how long you stayin?"

"Not long. Lissen. Me need yu help wid someting."

"Like what?"

"Well, I believe two days ago two box fulla gun and ammunition come to this estate and we need to know where and how we can get a hold of dem."

"By 'we' you mean the Maroons?"

"Yes. We need yu help. Did yu see any ting hush-hush happening day before yesterday?"

"Well, I did see some heavy lookin boxes like coffins put into the storage room under the great house where Backra store special rums and such. Is like a big cellar. You tink dey have guns?"

"Almost certain. We need a way to get a hold of dem."

"But the door is a heavy oak door with a big lock and a padlock on top of dat."

"Where is the keys dem?"

"Backra keep all the keys for the estate on a chain in him pants pocket. No way to tief dat because him use dem all de time. Is only when him go to Port Royal or Montego Bay him give the keys to Massa Jack and leave him in charge."

"How often him go to Port Royal?"

"Maybe once a month fi visit the whores dem. Him just come back from dere last week. And him hear dat Lord Stokes comin' fe a visit. De lawyer dem arrangin' everyting, but we have a whole heap a tings fe do."

"Is there anodder way into dat cellar?"

"Hmmm....ca'an tink of any right now. Wish I could help you."

"What room is jus' above the cellar?"

"The guest room where the lawyer or Reverend Heath stay when dey visit."

"Dat is the key."

Kwaku could hardly contain his excitement, and suggested they move to a less conspicuous locale to further their discussion.

"Hey you! What you doing here?"

It was Backra and he looked none too pleased. Kwaku modified his language in response:

"Pardon Boss. No offence. I just come to see if de missis need any ground provisions, sar. Me donkey carrying yam and cocoa and dasheen and potato and mangoes. I even have some callaloo, sar."

"So why are you talking to this brown gal?"

"I used to sell things to Reverend Heath in Port Royal when she was a young girl, sar. Just paying me respects, sar."

"Oh. I see. Go to the great house kitchen at the back. Missis is up there with the cooks. And you Poincie, back to work!"

Kwaku moved ever so slowly as he walked past an open window that revealed the interior of the living room, and approached the kitchen as one unsure of the layout of the area, as indeed he was, but also he could not help noticing the large weathered bastion of an oak door guarding the cellar. Yes, there was a huge padlock and a keyhole that would accommodate a key worthy of the locks at the Marshalsea prison. No. The risks were too great. Then he looked up to the second story at the window above. It was a plain window that could be thrown open to let in a breeze, unencumbered by the typical jalousies that graced the front facade of the house. Perhaps because this was the leeward side of the house, the jalousies were deemed unnecessary.

Before he took leave of the Stokes Estate he once more commiserated briefly with Poincie before going on his way.

"Look. It not good fe mek dem see we talk every time me come. But me want fe see you. What can we do?"

"Me wash de clothes in de river pon Friday mawnin. Come over to the trees and bush an you will see me by the river. You can hide Calypso in the bush."

"Good. See you next week, Putoos."

He would return in a week to see if the Missis needed any more ground provisions. Perhaps Missis had forgotten something he could supply? As he made his exit, Kwaku had the distinct feeling he was being watched.

He looked around to see Jack Hart observing him with some intensity. Kwaku tipped his cap in respect and intended to move on when Hart beckoned his interest to engage in conversation.

"What is your business here Mr..."

"Kwaku. Just call me Kwaku. I talk to Backra Bradford and the missis already, an me supply dem wid food, ground provisions and such. So, me just leavin.'"

"But you were talking to one of the servants."

"You mean Poincie? Yes, I know her from small when she was a young girl in Port Royal."

"And what is the nature of your friendship with her?"

"No offense, but why is dat a concern of yours?"

"Every time you come here you talk to her. Poincie works for me, and as her overseer I have a right to know what is going on with the workers and servants."

"She not doing a good job?"

"No, that's not it."

"Me get it. You have feelins fo her."

"Perhaps. But that is not anything of your concern."

"I admire you taste in women, Mr. Hart."

"So, you also have your eye on Poincie?"

"P'rhaps. And what if I do?"

"What do you have to offer a woman like Poincie? Aren't you out of your depth here? A farmer living in the bush? You see Poincie as a bush woman?"

"Now, wait a minute Jack Hart. You not much better dan a slave or indentured servant you'self. I am a freedman with no contract to fulfill and no obligation to anyone but meself. What make you tink you can offer her more dan me?"

"Poincie is a well-read woman. She is a very cultured young woman. She deserves a man with breeding and culture, not a farmer or laborer!"

"And you tink since you is a overseer dat you cultured and well-read? Don' mek me laugh!"

"It's no laughing matter. I..."

"Me get it. You white skin mek you qualified to court a mulatto, even if de mulatto better dan you in every way."

"Well, perhaps she is better than both of us, but I can offer her much more than you. Can't you see? If you love her, you should do what is best for her. Find yourself another woman more suitable."

"So dat she can be satisfied wid a unsuitable man who don't deserve her?"

"Look, Kwaku. I don't dislike you, but Poincie will sooner go after me than you. Let's face it. Every mulatto girl wants a white man."

"So you admit it, finally. So you will marry her and take her back to England and den what? How will your righteous father and mother feel 'bout their son marrying a colored woman? Be honest!"

Jack Hart hesitated, pondering a response. Kwaku continued.

"But you didn't plan to tek her back to England, did you? So Poincie was to be your convenience, your island girl, your bed-warmer? Something you cast aside when you move on to bigga and betta tings? Talk to me! If she was you sister and a man propose an arrangement like dat, would you be happy wid it?"

" I have genuine feelings for her!"

"Dat is what you tell yu'self so you won't feel too guilty when you tek advantage of her. You deceiving yu'self, but you can't fool me."

"You have no right to talk to me like that!"

"What you goin' do? Whip me? I will bust you ass wid de same whip and hang you wid it!"

Realizing that this discussion was generating more heat than light, Kwaku decided to leave and be on his way. He grabbed the rein of his donkey and left through the main gate and on to the main road.

CHAPTER TEN

Room for Intrigue

Word having been given of the imminent visit of Lord Stokes, Poincie asked if she might be of assistance in preparing the bedrooms for the visit. "De floors need polishing ma'am and de furniture need dusting. I could help if you need me ma'am." Mrs. Bradford was only too glad to delegate this responsibility to Poincie who did such an excellent job at her house, and she was told, at the house of the young assistant to her husband. "Start with the dusting Poincie, and then do the floors in Lord Stokes' chambers and then the guest rooms."

Kwaku would be back in a week. She had to act decisively, and quickly, hastening slowly to minimize suspicion. She would begin with Lord Stokes' chambers all right, but only initially, to satisfy the missis of her progress in preparing the rooms. Dusting completed in that area, she applied the polish to the floors but left the shining for later. She needed to inspect the floors in the guest room over the armory. She of course, dusted the room thoroughly, shining the chairs until they were mirror-like and the oval mirror likewise, but her greatest scrutiny was reserved for the floor. Truth be known, the rare occupancy of these rooms necessitated nothing more than a cursory sweeping and dusting, but stringent measures were needed to ensure the satisfaction of the great one when he arrived. Besides, the distinctive smell of the floor wax conveyed to any occupant the meticulous attention to every detail to ensure the satisfaction of the great Lord and his guests.

Poincie entered the guest room from the door upstairs. The walls were in paisley-patterned wallpaper with a dominance of bottle-green and accents of burgundy, tastefully done. At the far end of the room was the sash window and beside it the dresser complete with an ornate washbasin, matching goblet, and soap dish, and a towel bar at the side. Beside the dresser was a covered stool which when said cover was lifted revealed an oval opening under which a chimmy pot was positioned for the occupant's nocturnal convenience. To the left was an imposing wardrobe, two doors in deeply polished mahogany with wooden handles. Behind the open door of the bedroom to the right was the great iron bed in porcelain white and ornate ironwork bedhead decorated with ivory knobs and brass inserts. From a hook on the ceiling was suspended a streaming, sheer mosquito net which, though now gathered and tied at the end, could be unfurled to enclose the entire bed to fend off those night invaders. The bed faced the sash window and beside it was another window looking out on scrub and brush punctuating the landscape. The windows were fitted with identical curtains of semitransparent material patterned with faded roses.

It was a bright, well-lighted room at the corner of the house. Poincie had been in this room before but now inspected it with renewed interest. It was as one who had been away from home but returned to become reacquainted with familiar territory and enjoying the thrill of rediscovery.

The hardwood floors, deep in multiple layers of red ochre from many polishings, were neatly joined boards with nary a gap between them. From the intervals between the nails' heads Poincie determined that supporting the floorboards were beams three feet apart and at right angles (to use a term Reverend Heath had explained to her) to the floorboards. The boards themselves were in lengths of six feet. Her task became clearer: she would have to pry up those boards and then squeeze through a space of three feet and the width of perhaps four boards to gain access to the room below. Four boards. Those boards were in the middle of the room starting under the bed and ending under the windowsill. Where would she start? How could she lift them free? How could this be done without raising suspicion? She must not rearrange the furniture since this would not please the backra or his missis and might raise unwelcomed questions.

It took a few days to unobtrusively gather tools: a chisel, hammer, crowbar and spare nails salvaged from derelict furniture and which were suitably rusted. Edward, the estate carpenter had been a great help and sworn to silence. He was Kwaku's friend. He had been expecting Poincie as she approached him with her list of needs. He was only too thrilled to have Miss Poincie make her requests of him. He even volunteered to demonstrate to her how to use the tools but this she, to his disappointment, declined with a smile. It was a simple matter to bring these under her loose-fitting housedress by repeated trips to and from the room and secrete them under the bed-head in the guest room. However, time was limited and the longer those tools stayed there, the greater the risk of discovery. She could deny any knowledge of how they got there, but the searchlight would then shine on Edward and she had to protect him and the security of the entire operation. She must act soon.

Once the tools were assembled, she set to prying loose the molding at the base of the wall under the window. That exposed, the edge of the floorboards became visible, a gap of less than an inch but enough to use the crowbar to lift, with some effort, the edge of the first board. The board creaked as she lifted it to its full length, propping it up so as to avoid fully dislodging nails at the far end where it was secured. The second board was easier and the third. The resulting gap in the floor was adequate for her torso to slide through to the room below.

This was sufficient progress for now. She must replace everything in a manner that would leave no hint of the intrusion. The molding was simple enough and would cover the ends of the board where the nails were affixed, thus concealing them. Nails were put back in place with pressure rather than hammering. The floorboards were similarly restored to their original position and appearance, except for one board that had become wrenched free from its moorings by unyielding nails. Fortunately, this was barely evident because the boards ended under the foot of the great iron bed. Poincie tapped the nails into place with the hammerhead shrouded in thick cloth and smoothed out the edge of the wood as best she could, painfully lancing her fingers with splinters in the process.

Satisfied that she had laid the way for the next move, she walked away, but in doing so discovered another problem: the floor now creaked hideously. This wouldn't do. Ostensibly replenishing her floor polish, she went down the stairs, passed through the kitchen and engaged the cooks in conversation, and while passing a large crocus bag of cornmeal resting on the floor she scooped up a handful of the fine grain and deposited it in her pocket. On returning to her work upstairs, she gently sprinkled the cornmeal along the cracks between the floorboards, working the grain in and testing each board. Then she swept the area clean. The cornmeal worked. She walked away with nary a complaint from the floor.

It was evening and a feeling of pleasant fatigue came over Poincie as she reclined on her bed in the one small room she occupied on the ground floor of the great house. She recalled the days and nights under the care of Gatha and Reverend Heath. Kwaku had told her that Gatha was now showing some evidence of the passage of the years. So was Reverend Heath who had been the only father she ever knew. Parishioners had often called him "father" but in a special way she thought of him as her foster father, her protector, her nurturer, spiritual advisor, educator. He had opened to her a window on the outside world far beyond Port Royal, of kings and princes, fairy tales, Bible stories, politics, history, economics and cultures far away and long ago. His gentle manner, even his occasional reprimand, was in such a loving, tactful, diplomatic way as to leave her self-esteem intact. His treatment of her and Gatha elicited a deep and abiding affection for him. Poincie felt a loyalty and appreciation for the man who provided for her the only home she ever knew.

She reminisced about Kwaku who had become to her such a dear friend and the many stories he entertained her with and the way he humored her childlike curiosity and answered her questions. She owed so much to these three people, each of whom had played a major role in shaping the young woman she had become. The Maroon, the Englishman, and the devoted native woman had all left their mark on her development.

She recalled how Gatha had told of children growing up in the country and the games the children played when work on the plantation was over for the day. Gatha had told of how the children collected many Peenie Wallies in a clear quart bottle and how these fireflies emitted a glow bright enough to light one's path through the narrow footpaths at night. Peenie Wallies! That was the answer to a problem. How could she see into the dark dungeon of an armory to accomplish her mission? A lighted torch was too risky. Fire and gunpowder in close proximity was not a good idea. A torch could be readily extinguished if necessary to avoid detection but then how could it be discretely relit? Peenie Wallies was the answer.

The next night she collected the Peenie Wallies. A quart bottle would hold enough of the glowing beetles to provide adequate light. Poincie covered the bottle with a black cloth and simply opened it when she needed light. It was time to complete this part of the mission. Now she must find a way to lower herself through the narrow opening and bring up the guns and gunpowder. She strung two ropes through the mouths of two crocus bags and lowered the bags through the opening after tying knots at intervals along the length of the rope and then tying the rope ends, one to the foot of the dresser in the room and the other to the foot of the wardrobe.

Then she lowered herself by those same ropes by gripping the knots. Holding the light aloft, she noticed that the boxes had been pried open, no doubt to satisfy Backra's curiosity, and included both muskets and gunpowder. She filled the bags, climbed up the ropes and hauled up the loot after herself into the guest room above. It took several such trips in quick succession.

Poincie noticed that the wardrobe had a key in one of its two doors. She tried the key in the other door and it worked there also. She would use the wardrobe as a holding place for the guns and ammunition until they could be moved to a safer location to be collected by Kwaku or the Maroons. She locked the muskets and gunpowder keg in the wardrobe and placed the key above in the recessed area above the wardrobe. Extrication of the loot would have to be through one of the side windows, possibly to the one at the side of the house near the woods and bushy area.

Poincie gingerly replaced the floorboards, reinserted the nails and re-covered the ends of the boards with the base molding under the window. She tested the planks for squeaks, and, satisfied that the room looked completely undisturbed, she carried the coconut brush, the polish and a dust cloth down the stairs with her. On her way down, she was met with the sight of Mrs. Bradford at the foot of the stairs, arms akimbo, observing her descent.

"What you doing up there so late Poincie?"

"Jus finishin' the last likkle bit of cleaning an dustin' ma'am. De room dem ready now ma'am." Poincie made sure the bottle was safely in a pocket of her ample dress, but the coconut brush, dusting cloth (which had covered the bottle as needed), and the polish container were obvious. She lifted them briefly to punctuate her explanation.

"Good work, Poincie." Mrs. Bradford left through the main entrance returning to her own abode for the night. Poincie swept her forefinger over her forehead, flashed the sweat to the side and entered her own room, collapsing on the bed. Sometime later she would hear those same words, "Good work Poincie," this time from Kwaku accompanied by a heart-warming hug of appreciation.

CHAPTER ELEVEN

Wash Day at Stokes Hall

Kwaku and Calypso made their way through the thicket of trees toward the river guided by the waving clumps of bamboo that typically flanked so many streams. Soon he came across a footpath, the red soil tamped firm and smooth by many footsteps over the years and found a small clearing with grass between the trees. Here he tethered Calypso and relieved him of the weight of the hampers, leaving him to graze and enjoy the shade. Kwaku took the footpath to the river where he knew Poincie would be waiting.

As he approached he began to hear the gurgling of the river as the water skipped over the small rocks worn smooth by the water's constant caresses. Above, he was conscious of the soughing of the trees and he broke into the clearing where the canopy of arched bamboo trees swayed gently in the breeze as the sun played hide-and-seek with the grass. The silver sash of water made its way through the flat grass interrupted by a few partially submerged rocks scattered here and there on the riverbed, their tops above the water like bathers at a resort.

He saw her first. She had just set her basket down on the riverbank and had just begun to step over the stones to a point where she could sit on one rock and scrub the clothes on a nearby rock already worn smooth by many washings. She had gathered her skirt and tucked it between her thighs to keep it dry while her feet rested in the water as she prepared to begin her task. Kwaku cupped his hands, his thumbs held together to leave a narrow gap, and blew a familiar two-note sound. Immediately Poincie looked up with a smile on her face and tried to focus on the underbrush from the direction of the sound. Kwaku emerged and trotted over to the riverbank across from her. She had already skipped to the bank and the two hugged, kissing each other on the cheeks.

"Hey! You have work me dear. Mek me help."

"You crazy. We can talk same time me do me work."

"No, you wash and me rinse and put de wet clothes in de basket."

"Awright."

They set to work with Poincie taking each piece of clothing, rubbing it with a block of carbolic soap and then scrubbing, squishing the garment in such a way that the expelled soapy water gave a crisp, sharp splurge of a sound that amused Kwaku. He loved to watch her smooth but strong fingers work the clothes. She tossed each piece at him and he caught it with lightning reflexes, they being in close proximity to each other. Soon the last piece was tossed at Kwaku and he rinsed it and placed it in the basket. They so enjoyed each other's company that they were surprised that the clothes were finished so soon, long before they had tired of catching up on the happenings both at Stokes Hall and at Port Royal and at Reverend Heath's in particular.

Kwaku had a paper sack from which he brought out some naseberries, mangoes, and Otaheiti apples, and Poincie's favorite, sweet sop fruit. That reminded Poincie that she had brought in the pocket of her skirt a neatly wrapped piece of Kwaku's favorite treat, sweet potato pudding. As they enjoyed the goodies they recalled how Aunt Gatha used to make the potato pudding in a cast iron pot set on three large stones on the ground with firewood between the stones. On the iron pot cover she heaped red hot coals so that there was heat from above and heat below to bake the pudding. Poincie recalled how Aunt Gatha used to say this was " Hell a-top, hell a-bottom, and hallelujah in the middle!" They both laughed until they almost choked on the pudding they were eating.

"Aunt Gatha really miss you."

"Me miss her too, and Reverend Heath."

"Dey miss you too and talk 'bout you all de time."

"And how about you?"

" Me worry about you sometime."

"For why?"

"You are a good lookin' woman, Poincie."

"Thank you Kwaku, but why would dat worry you so?"

"The backras and de odder man dem will be afta you."

"I can handle myself Kwaku. Don't worry 'bout me."

"It would mash me up if anyting happen to you."

They were sitting side by side on the riverbank. She leaned her cheek on his left shoulder, her hand grasping his bicep and he, ever so lightly, reached over with his right hand and caressed her cheek with the back of his hand. They sat wordlessly, listening to each other breathe, comfortable in the silence. Kwaku remembered that on one of his visits to the Heath residence in Port Royal he had noticed that one of the trees in the backyard had an abundance of the Cuscuta or "dodder" vine growing on the limbs of the tree. He had smiled when he saw this. Young girls called this stringy yellow creeper the "love bush." They believed that if they take a small piece of the vine, throw it onto the limb of a tree and called out the name of the one they love, then if the vine grew their love would grow, but if it withered and died, then so would their love for each other. Did Poincie have a boyfriend? Kwaku chuckled to himself. Poincie, sensing his inner chuckle by the vibrations of his belly, asked, "What?"

"You remember when you were just a young girl?"

"Yes."

"You remember de love bush in de tree in de backyard?"

"Goodness gracious! You remember dat?"

Poincie let go of Kwaku's arm and lay back on the grass laughing at the folly of her youth. Kwaku leaned back sideways to rest on his elbow, looked down at her and laughed too. When their laughter subsided Kwaku asked, "So, who was de boyfriend at de time? Who name did you call out when you throw de love bush?"

Poincie looked up at Kwaku, her eyes with pleading tenderness: "Who you tink, Kwaku? Is long time now me love you."

"Oh Poincie..." Kwaku leaned down, touched her chin with his forefinger and brought his lips to hers. Her moist mouth parted to accept his, the quick, shallow puffs of breath from her nose caressing the side of his face as their tongues met and slid over each other, again and again, each savoring slippery bliss as Poincie felt and heard Kwaku's murmured Hmmm...as they kissed, prolonging the thrill until it seemed their souls merged. They both went limp, falling back on the grass holding hands and looking up at the bamboo cathedral above them.

CHAPTER TWELVE

Catch a Fire

George Bradford looked up from the rice-and-peas with brown-stewed chicken in front of him as his eye caught the yellow flicker of flame against the windowpane at the far end of his dining room. Thinking it might be merely the hues of a sunset, he turned his attention once more to the meal on his plate. That persistent flash of color on the windowpane. Sunsets don't normally show rapid flickers of color. That must be a fire. Fire in the cane fields? Damn! Just then Jack Hart burst into the room in a state of alarm. Both men parted the curtains and confirmed their worst suspicions. The west side of the plantation was on fire, the evening sky ablaze with the cane, each stalk like a torch brightening up the evening. They heard distant crackling and popping as sparks ascended to the sky, like so many fireflies lifted by the wind.

"Did you order the flaming of the cane?"

"Of course not. I thought you did."

"That cane needs two more weeks to mature before harvesting. We agreed to flame it then!"

"I tell you I did not order the burn!"

"Damn it man! Get the hell over there with all hands! This is not London where we call the Fire Brigade!"

Bradford and the servants summoned the laborers in the slave quarters. They were just about to have their evening meal when someone pointed in the direction of the west side and noted the flaming sky. This was no controlled burn, the kind one does before a harvest. This fire was out of control.

Bradford organized all hands to form a bucket relay from the large catchment tank behind the Bradford house and a pond nearer the fire. They used pots, pans, buckets and anything that could carry water, passing these containers from hand to hand so that a steady stream of water was dumped on the fire. The fire raged on. The cane field fire had developed a will of its own that seemed to defy the feeble efforts of human beings and would only dissipate when it was good and ready. Bradford watched and shouted orders punctuated by cussing as he watched their feeble efforts in the face of an angry inferno. The heat was unbearable even from a respectable distance and Jack had stripped off his shirt as he joined in passing the water toward the front. In the intermittent light and dark of a fire he was sometimes indistinguishable from the slaves he ruled.

Meanwhile Bradford had visions of Lord Stokes arriving and looking over the burnt-out remnants of his great house. The prospect haunted him and lent a keen sense of urgency to his pacing and yelling of orders. That some slaves may take this opportunity to escape to the hills was another possible outcome of this emergency, but he would not allow himself to be distracted by that prospect. He must save the buildings while limiting the extent to which the fire would destroy the cane fields.

Bradford recalled explaining to Jack that controlled burns were a common occurrence on a plantation. When the cane was about to be harvested the workers would set sections on fire and progressively cover the desired harvest area until the process was complete. The flames stripped the cane stalks of the long lacerating leaves and rendered the stalks much easier to cut and trim, while small animals, tarantulas, and snakes would be flushed out or incinerated. The resulting ashes would also be beneficial to the soil for the next crop of sugar cane.

Had someone prematurely set the cane field on fire? Was this an accident? Sabotage? Did Jack Hart mess up his duties again? Bradford did not know what to think. In any case, what was most important was to get this fire under control before the great house and the other structures were themselves threatened. To Bradford's dismay, the smoke was blowing in the direction of the great house and the wind seemed to be intensifying.

He recalled that not many months before the overseer at the nearby Hampton Estates was at supper with guests when one asked about the putt-putt sound coming from the roof of the farmhouse. "It's nothing of concern" they were told, "just the pecking of birds feeding on the seeds fallen on the roof from the limbs of a tree." Soon the putt-putt became a crackling and a popping and before long the roof caved in fully aflame, and the entire house collapsed in a great conflagration, with the occupants barely escaping with their lives. The damned Maroons had shot arrows onto the roof, each arrow made of kandia wood that had natural oils and retained a flame until it impacted the thatched roof of the house. Bradford scanned the roofs of his cottage and that of the great house. No flame. But if this sugarcane fire was not contained the result could very well be the same.

The sickly-sweet smell of sugarcane mingled with the burning flesh and hair of rodents caught in the blaze blew across the field. The orange-yellow flames licked ever higher giving rise to a stifling smoke as hot air burned the nostrils of the fire fighters. It soon became clear to Bradford that their efforts were futile in the face of the advancing conflagration. The water poured on the fire reached only the periphery of the flames and merely added a steamy smokiness to the already miserable cauldron of heat, smoke, smells, and flames. A new strategy was needed or all would be lost.

Bradford ordered the bucket brigade to stop. He assigned a half a dozen slaves, mostly women, to watch the great house and the cottages for flying embers reaching their roofs, and to direct the water to those structures if they saw any roof threatened. Then he called for all hands to be issued machetes to cut a swath of cane leaving a gap of some twelve feet and thus halt the forward march of the fire toward the buildings. He would restrict the fire to a circle and let it burn itself out.

Other hands were assigned to watch for any breach of the line if the breeze carried embers over the line to the rest of the cane field. The burn area seemed like one giant torch with cane stalks mere strands in the fabric of a wick reaching skyward, but gradually that flame subsided, diminished gradually, until mere embers remained among the bare standing stalks of sugar cane. The strategy worked.

It was after midnight when Bradford called an end to the firefighting. He would have the burned out cane stalks, not yet at full maturity or sweetness, gathered nevertheless and sent to the grinders and thus minimize the extent of the loss. He also ordered no change in the early morning routine, save for harvesting the burn area. He retired for the night angry, his head swirling with scenarios of how this had happened and how he should deal with it.

Bradford summoned Jack to his house the next morning.

"That fire was deliberately set. You know that, of course?"

"Of course, but by whom?"

"Does that matter? What matters is that the sabotage must not go unpunished!"

"Interrogate the slaves?"

"They'll lie through their teeth every one of them! Sons of whores!"

"Then what will we do?"

"Punish one as an example."

"I see. But what if we punish the wrong one?"

"Damn! Are you so dense? The one who is punished will know who was the true cause of the punishment and will take his revenge on the true perpetrator. As long as they fight among themselves they don't have time to rebel against us. That's how it works. Gosh! You are so naïve sometimes! Any of the bastards give you trouble lately?"

Jack thought of the time he overheard Johnny snidely refer to the "walk-foot backra" and could hear the stifled snickering of the slaves behind his back. He didn't appreciate the demeaning arrogance of a mere slave.

"No, but that fellow, the axe boy at the mill house, stands like he thinks he is a chief back in Africa, and the others look up to him. I was thinking of sending him back to the fields last week after he held my stare longer than necessary. Insolent brute!"

"Enough said. His name is Johnny. Tomorrow morning I will deal with this brute."

CHAPTER THIRTEEN

Shock and Disgust

As usual, Jack Hart had arisen with the crowing of the rooster. After breakfast served by a maid from Bradford's house, he rode his mule to where the field hands were all assembled in a clearing beside the house. Arriving somewhat late, he noticed that the crestfallen Negroes were more subdued than usual. It wasn't the early hour that rendered them extraordinarily morose, nor yet the fatigue that even a night's sleep could not entirely ameliorate. Everyone there knew that this gathering was to mete out a punishment in which vicariously every slave would participate.

It was time to make a public example of a saboteur. Indeed, the first phase of the punishment had already been undertaken with Bradford earlier in the morning. He had ridden over to the slave quarters and summoned Johnny from his hut, immediately flailing him with the cat-o-nine from atop his horse as he corralled him with the help of two drivers to the present site, no explanation offered.

Jack noticed Johnny on the ground. He was flat on his back, spread-eagled with wrists and ankles tied securely to large pegs embedded in the ground. The battered, shredded heads of the pegs testified to the depth to which they were driven into the ground and the stout ropes by which he was bound rendered his wrists numb so that he couldn't flex his fingers. His ankles were abrased with rope burns. Two pegs on each side of his head restricted any movement there. Jack noticed that his mouth had been pried open and hyperextended by means of two short rods with notched ends that separated his upper and lower rows of teeth. Johnny could not move his mouth or lips.

It was clear that before his arrival the negro had been viciously whipped, no doubt by the Backra or one of the drivers on the estate. The cat-o-nine-tails had left bloody streaks across his torso and some wounds were still oozing blood. His belly rose and fell in desperate gasps for breath as the only expression of his pain. The rapid expiration of breath from his throat punctuated the desperate breathing with a hacking, grating sound.

At this point the Backra, pacing around with a long musket and a whip stuck in his waistband, motioned to one of the Negroes who, eyes averted, stood on the outskirts of the huddled group.

"You! You! Over here!"

The slave timidly approached the backra.

"Drop you pants."

He did as he was told.

"And you drawers."

He complied.

"Now squat over his face."

He did as ordered.

"Now, shit in his mouth!"

The slave exerted himself, hesitantly at first, then in compliance as Johnny gagged and heaved, half stifled in this misery and ultimate disgrace. Onlookers averted their eyes but could not occlude their nostrils. A fixed, crooked half-smile was on Backra's face and Jack turned away, repulsed by the awful scene he now felt complicit in carrying out and by the smug, sadistic visage of George Bradford. Jack Hart himself felt chastened by the harrowing scene he had just witnessed. The slave was left thus until midday when it was determined that further exposure would endanger his life through complications of sunstroke and respiratory distress. Lord Stokes would not take kindly to the loss of his livestock should the young slave die.

Later that afternoon, Bradford paid Jack a visit.

"So you couldn't handle this morning's proceedings Mr. Hart?" He glared at him with contempt.

"I found it unsavory, to be honest. Never saw such cruelty in all my life."

"Damn it man! You are here to seek a fortune like all of us! What the hell is wrong with you?"

"I'm just thinking that my father in England would be shocked by the cruelty I have witnessed here."

"He would be shocked but also delighted by the fortune you could amass by being here. Look, they outnumber us fifteen to one. We have to keep them in check by treating them like the animals they are. Give them an inch and they would take a mile. They would slit our throats at the least opportunity. We are walking a tightrope here, and the balance pole is the army, the militia and brute force. Make no bones about that!"

"But it's not Christian!"

"Christian my arse! You don't know your Bible? The folks tell me that in the book of Leviticus it says you can whip a slave to within an inch of his life and it's fine because he is your property. That is the word of God! After God saved the Israelites from Egyptian slavery, one of the first things he told them was to enslave the Canaanites and take their land. Anyway, that is what they tell me. It's do it to them before they do it to you. That's the Bible! So don't get on your high horse with me about cruelty! Jackass!"

"I never realized you were a man of the Good Book," Jack responded somewhat cynically. "Don't patronize me Hart! I can have you whipped just as easily as that slave. Your arse is mine until your contract is fully discharged."

Bradford continued. "Look at the damn Beckfords! The pompous members of the House of Beckford were nothing more than mere cloth-cutters in England. Invested a little money in slaves and sugar here in Jamaica. Look at them today! Lord Byron calls Beckford 'England's richest son.' And how? His brother William runs the plantations over in Westmoreland and sends the money to his brother in London. They are rolling in wealth. They are the new aristocrats. Word has it that Beckford will be the next Lord Mayor of London.

"And you expect the same results today?"

"Damn it man. Can't you see? We are sitting on a gold mine and you have this foolish notion of cruelty and this warped sense of justice. You have a lot to learn, and you better learn fast. Damn you!"

George Bradford stomped away incensed that Jack had brought to the surface a truth that he had chosen to bury deep in his dark psyche and now had bared in the scorching light of day.

Jack Hart stood staring at the ground, thoroughly browbeaten, as Bradford stalked away.

CHAPTER FOURTEEN

Clearing the Fog

Poincie tried to sort out the convoluted tangle of feelings inside her. The fire had deprived most of a good night's sleep and her mind was lethargic in its attempt to untangle her conflicted emotions. Her mission had been successfully completed. At the height of the fire she was not on the scene, but everyone would have assumed that she was one of many shadowy figures passing water from hand to hand, one of many scurrying figures, frantically doing their part in this emergency.

No one would have seen her lowering sacks through the open side window on the upper floor of the great house to the ground outside, or thereafter noticed the stealthy movements of male figures whose black bodies were obscured by the deepening darkness of the nightfall and the thick brush which obscured their movements. No one noticed the conveyance of crocus bags to the edge of the estate where a certain donkey and its owner galloped away for the hills far away from the torched stalks of a sugarcane field on fire.

When later the firefighters continued their efforts, Poincie was there passing buckets of water to douse the fire, just as they all assumed she had been doing all along. She felt some satisfaction for the key role she played in striking a blow for justice. On the other hand, she felt a pang of guilt because she realized that her actions were partially responsible for a slave named Johnny to be horribly humiliated and tortured for a crime he did not commit. She wished there was some way for her to compensate him for the horror she had caused him. But how could she risk his wrath if he discovered her role in his punishment? And was she not in some way also working for his cause? Do not all concerned have a role to play, a sacrifice to render for the overall good of the many? She knew that some Maroons had set the fire and that Kwaku and others had spirited the weapons and ammunition away after she dropped them through the window from the room she so carefully cleaned and used to hide the cache.

Furthermore, she was still at risk. When would Bradford realize that half of the guns and ammunition was missing? Would he divine how they were taken without the door and lock being disturbed? Would the fact that she took equally from both boxes lower the risk of his discovery of the theft as she hoped?

Clara, a young house servant approached Poincie.

"A word wid you please, Miss Poincie."

"Yes?"

"Miss Poincie, please be careful because Backra Jack can mek life hard fe you."

"What you mean? Massa Jack is a nice man."

"I mean him can get wicked when him ready. De odder day him tell Backra Bradford dat Johnny do sumpn' bad an you see what happen to him."

"You mean Johnny haffe suffer 'cause Massa Jack tell sumpn pon him?"

"Yes, Miss Poincie."

"How come you know dis?"

"Jus de odder day me hear Backra Bradford a talk to Backra Jack and ask who set de cane piece on fire. Dem neva know who do it, but Massa Jack say Johnny should be punish 'cause him too uppity. Dem neva know say me a lissen while me was a clean and give dem tea."

"Thank you my dear. If you hear anything more, you come tell me, hear?"

"Yes, Miss Poincie."

Poincie was down on her knees cleaning the floor when Jack returned to his dwelling. This time she did not engage in the rhythmic exercise of polishing with the coconut brush. She was strangely silent, pensive, apparently unaware of his arrival on the scene. Her brush strokes carried a rather lethargic, even funereal cadence that betrayed her inner turmoil and sadness.

She thought how ludicrous Europeans could be in their minds: Did they understand that the same ears tuned to heed their every beck and call and fill their every need could also hear their public conversations albeit in their drawing rooms and dining areas? Did they relegate slaves to such nonentity that spoken words in earshot didn't matter if they fell on slave ears? In any case, she was grateful when Clara related to her the conversation between Backra Bradford and Massa Jack. So Jack had fingered Johnny as prime suspect in the cane burning.

"Hello, Poincie."

"Hello."

"Is something the matter?"

"Nuthin."

"But you're not singing while you work today. Tired?"

"Tired of dis life." Poincie continued her shining of the floor uninterruptedly.

"Anything in particular?"

"Nuthin dat should concern yu."

"If it concerns you, Poincie, then it is of some concern to me."

Poincie could hold out no longer. The floodgates were breached and out she blurted:

"Massa Jack. Yu not like dem. Don' mek dem change yu! For a human to treat anodder like a beast, him mus become less dan human too. Him must become like a beast, an animal himself!"

"So this is what this is about? The punishment of Johnny? He deserved it!"

"How come he deserved dat kind of treatment? No animal deserve to be treated like dat!"

"It was necessary to punish him because we have reason to believe that he had something to do with the fire yesterday."

"What did Johnny do? Tell me!"

"There are many things I cannot explain to you Poincie. You would not understand."

"Is not dat I can't understan'. Is dat you can't explain. Yu name is Hart but you heartless."

"In any case this conversation is over." Jack Hart stalked out of the room, slamming the door behind him.

Poincie, still seething, thought of Jack Hart as a living contradiction, sweet and thoughtful, but naïve and increasingly corrupted by the system of which he had become both perpetrator and victim. How could he come from places so far away and still be so unaware of the larger world issues confronting him and the people above and below him in the hierarchy of Jamaican social life? Isn't it ironic that she had to acquaint the young backra with the stark realities that surrounded him? He seemed physically present on the island but in a schizophrenic manner his soul was back in England. Yet he came to the island to make something of himself because he had no way of doing so in his native land. On the other hand, he hated what he had to become to make it on the island. Poor Jack Hart was "a house divided against itself," as Reverend Heath would say.

Poincie recalled the first time she, as a young girl had seen the young backra. Gatha and herself were at the market in Port Royal one day when a vessel arrived and all eyes turned toward the docks. Out of sheer curiosity, she and Gatha had gone to watch its arrival and the people disembarking. Among them was this baby-faced young massa looking wide-eyed and lost before the backra had hailed him and took him off to, as Poincie later learned, the Stokes Hall Estate. Later, by coincidence she was assigned to be a house worker on the estate. It was obvious to Poincie that Massa Jack was from a humble background like so many other book-keepers and overseers, all come to the island to make their fortune and not much better than slaves themselves. Massa Jack did not ride a horse but would soon have one like any proper Englishman. Backra would eventually see to that. In the meanwhile, he was referred to, behind his back, as "the walk-foot backra."

She liked the baby-faced young Englishman, but refused to be caught up in his conflicting dilemma of contradictory values. He was nothing but conflict and trouble. She must maintain her distance.

CHAPTER FIFTEEN

The Rendezvous

Jack Hart was startled at his own realization. This was another Friday. It was the day Poincie went to the river to wash the clothes of the Bradford household. She customarily chose to wash during the morning hours to allow the midday sun to dry the clothes that she hung on a line behind the Bradford house. She would pass close by Jack's humble abode on the footpath that led to the cluster of trees and bamboo marking the proximity of the river and the waterfall that Jack had seen on his initial tour of the estate.

Today, he would follow her on foot from a distance. If she discovered his presence he would feign some pretext of inspection and pass it off as mere coincidence.

He didn't have long to wait. From behind the half-closed jalousie he saw her coming with a large round basket of clothes piled high and balanced on her head. As she disappeared into the underbrush, half-stooping to allow the basket to clear overhanging branches, Jack followed. He knew he would not lose her. The footpath, well defined by frequent use, would lead him to her. The thicket and the path through it were elbows-wide, close and winding, and often Jack could see the basket disappear around a bend and he knew he was as yet undiscovered. At first he could hear the white noise of falling water. Then as she entered a clearing the sound of the waterfall and river grew louder. Jack halted, choosing to use the cover of the jungle as he observed her. He stepped off the path and leaned against a large cotton tree from which he, hidden between the high buttress roots, could see her clearly.

Poincie set her basket on the ground amid the low grass on the banks of the river. Twenty yards behind her a promontory loomed like a backdrop over which the river merrily spilled its drapery of water twenty feet down a cascade of rocks where it formed a natural pool of expanding concentric ripples. The river was shielded from the sun by a canopy of overarching bamboo that resulted in a subdued light except for the random sheath of light created when the breeze shifted the bamboo and admitted shafts of brilliant sunshine that danced on the gurgling river and the dark green grass. Close to her basket and a few feet from the bank was a cluster of rocks protruding from the surface of the river. Some of these rocks showed the bleached weathered look that came from their surfaces being used as a scrubbing surface for numerous loads of clothes.

Poincie set to work. Wetting each item of clothing in the water, she rubbed it with a large cake of carbolic soap, scrubbed it on the sloping surface of the rock and set it aside on a nearby rock. Later she rinsed each piece in the river, wrung it free of excess water, and expertly tossed it back into the basket on the bank. Wearing a loose frock, Poincie attacked her task with gusto. Her unrestrained breasts jiggled under the rhythm of her vigorous scrubbing and her strong arms glistened with sweat. Jack watched from his vantage point of the large cotton tree, wondering if he should reveal himself and perhaps engage her in conversation. This was another setting in which to observe her at work and he liked what he saw.

Besides, he had always enjoyed engaging Poincie in conversation when she came to work at his house. It seemed that she had had free access to a wide range of reading material, thanks to Reverend Heath who had taught her to read. She conversed with Jack on topics that he himself, an Englishman, was surprised to find that anyone in the Indies, let alone a near-slave would know. Theology, British history, some politics and even some economics were topics on which Jack learned a great deal just from conversing with Poincie. Furthermore, she challenged his conscience on matters of colonial dominance and the perceived evils of the slave trade. No woman on the estate, not even Mrs. Bradford, could or would converse on such matters. Gradually he came to see Poincie as not just a servant or a prospect for sexual conquest but a confidant who helped him pass the tedium of plantation life with stimulating banter.

Jack noticed that on those occasions when they engaged in conversation she partially abandoned her patois for a more sophisticated, English-tinged mode of communication which, melded with her native inflections, he found charming, even amusing. He delighted in her exchanges with him not only for the issues being discussed, but also for the novelty of her expression.

What he couldn't understand and what bothered him was the way she demurely but unmistakably spurned every physical advance he made toward her. Reaching out to touch her hand while they talked around the tiny dining table, a subtle brushing of their bodies when they both passed through the doorway, a hug declined when they laughed together on the porch: all discretely avoided. Didn't she know that a mulatto woman like herself always sought out young white men such as he as benefactors and lovers? Wasn't having a baby by a white man a way to ensure some support for the child and mother? Wasn't this one way of "raising the color" of the offspring and thus moving up the ladder of Jamaican society? Surely she must know this! Did she avoid closeness with him because of his status as an assistant overseer? Did she see him as simply an oppressive Englishman? In anger she had described him as heartless. Did she actually believe so?

His was a temporary situation. He would make his fortune and leave all this behind, a necessary evil but not endured long enough to change the person he knew himself to be. People did unpleasant things of necessity. People went to war, a nasty business. They executed criminals, a necessary business. It didn't define them. In another generation it was all forgotten and the spoils of necessary evil could be enjoyed without further repercussion. How could Poincie understand this?

The Beckfords in London had no idea of the cost of their good fortune. No one asked how many hours of slave labor provided the fancy china plate Lord Beckford held aloft to the amazement of his guests, the fancy paintings that adorned every wall in his mansion. Besides, there was always the

Bible and its endorsement of slavery....Well, this was a nasty business, this whole idea of sugar, slaves, and the colonies, but who was he to judge all these people? Didn't slavery exist in every civilization? It was a human thing, after all. Some of the freed natives themselves said, "I am here to drink milk. I am not here to count cows."

At this moment Jack heard a yell and looked up to see a looming figure atop the waterfall just as the figure dove into the pool with a loud splash. Poincie was startled and turned around in alarm, only to burst into a laugh of recognition as the figure surfaced and, wiping his face, flashed a row of white teeth and scooped a spray of water in Poincie's direction. Jack did not at first recognize the intruder, but clearly Poincie did not regard him thusly. He swam and waded down to her cluster of rocks and grabbed her playfully from behind, cupping both her breasts and kissing her neck. Poincie squirmed and gently chided him and resumed her task with a half-smile on her face.

Sitting on the rock behind her, the slave, for so he appeared to Jack, encircled her waist with both arms as she finished the last few garments, gradually slipping his hands down to her knees, up under her dress, and sliding them up toward where her thighs converged. She slapped his hands away and elbowed him backwards into the water. She skipped on protruding stones over to the bank of the river and proceeded to arrange the garments for transport in the basket. He soon joined her there, slapping Poincie on her bottom with a wet towel and on his second swipe Poincie grabbed the towel as they proceeded to wrestle on the grass. Jack's first impulse was to rescue Poincie, but it was obvious that this was not the first encounter between these two.

Suddenly Jack recalled where he had seen the man. It was the door-to-door donkey man who sometimes supplied Mrs. Bradford with ground provisions. This was the brute that now fondled Poincie? What was his name? Jack seemed to recall hearing a house slave call him Kwaku. Kwaku. Yes, that was his name, the name he gave when they had had their heated argument.

With his hand around Poincie's waist Kwaku steered her toward Jack's hiding place by the large cotton tree. What the hell? Should he cough and reveal himself? How would he explain his presence? Jack would have thought that a large cotton tree would have been the last place for an assignation like this. Natives believed that duppies resided under cotton trees. Their fear of ghosts would have made this a taboo place, but Kwaku and Poincie seemed unmindful of the superstition. Giggling and feigning reluctance, Poincie allowed him to drag her to a large space between the sloping buttress roots on the opposite side of the tree.

But be still. This could be acutely embarrassing. He could pretend he had fallen asleep between roots of the cotton tree if they discovered him.

Torn between intrigue and disgust, he was a jumble of emotions that both energized and immobilized him into enduring the torture of his soul. Poincie's weak protests grew weaker, her giggles less audible until they gave way to an audible sigh of surrender, and Kwaku groaned with satisfaction as he savored his conquest. Jack felt the rush of blood to his head and to his loins simultaneously. The surge of blood at his temples was as audible to him as the breeze rustling the foliage overhead. Indeed, at times he could not distinguish between his own head sounds and the rapid intermittent breathing and moaning of the two on the other side of the tree. Only the occasional urgent aspirations of sucked breaths between the teeth differentiated his perverse responses from theirs.

They seemed oblivious to all else but their own pleasure, giving free reign to vocalizations of delight and passion, mingled whimpers and deep groans, occasionally muffled by the breeze and the sounds of the cascading waterfall. Then the chatter of birds that began overhead was persistent and incessant while stout buttress roots and waving branches, limbs swayed and leaves joined in one natural upheaval with the chorus of the river laughing on its way. Then the birds in unison exploded into dispersion as they soared high into the air, scattering in every direction. How had he got himself into this predicament? How would he exit with his pride and dignity intact? His ordeal seemed interminable!

And then the leaves were still and only the gurgling of the river was perceptible. He heard a deep sigh of release from the opposite side of the tree. And another. The two, sensing the passage of time, hastened to resume a normal routine. Kwaku helped Poincie to lift the basket, now heavier than before the washing, onto her head, and she retraced her steps through the bush from which she would eventually emerge into the full sunlight. She would approach the clotheslines with her basket as she usually did. Kwaku returned from the direction from whence he came.

Jack, his heart galloping and his mind a confusion of emotions, collapsed momentarily in his hiding place before composing himself and returning to his abode, but not before noting Kwaku's exit through the main gate, leading his donkey. Yes, he said to himself with teeth clenched and fists tight as crocodile jaws. He must watch that nigga son of a whore more closely.

So these two were together. She had given herself to this Kwaku. She had the audacity to reject him in favor of a common laborer. She had chosen to be with a nigga instead of a white man who could promise her a future and lift her to a higher social position in Jamaica. He who was a supervisor on the plantation on which she worked was cast aside as if he didn't matter. Were she in England she would be no more privileged than a servant emptying chamber pots. She must pay for her insolence. He would not rest until she paid dearly. He would see to it.

CHAPTER SIXTEEN

A Hurricane

Gatha stood in front of the black wood-burning stove, nudged the logs tighter together and kneaded her right hip with a folded fist. That pain again. She looked out through the smoky window at the narrow strip of sky afforded by her view. Very little blue. The sky was brooding, morose. Towering cumulus clouds moved stealthily, menacingly across the dark canvas of grey sky. She could tell it was going to rain. She noticed Reverend Heath wending his way out through the gate and rushed to him with a folded umbrella.

"Yu will need dis, sar."

"Nonsense! The weather is overcast but it's fine!" Gatha thought how this kind of weather was fine compared to what the reverend was used to in England, from what she was told, but for Jamaica this was not good.

"Yes sar. Fine for now. Before you come home it goin' rain, sar."

"Oh. all right. If you say so." Gatha knew he had learned that her instincts, or whatever that was, was more often than not correct, although he begrudgingly accepted the proffered umbrella and went his way, using it as a walking stick like a proper English gentleman.

That pain again. Worse this time. Gatha gathered the garments off the clothesline. She wished she had Poincie to help her reach up when the pain in her hip got this bad, but Poincie was over at Stokes Hall. She had been sent there as a helper at the Stokes Hall Estate. She thought it was a pity that Poincie had to settle for being a housemaid even though, thanks to Reverend Heath, she could read and write as well as any overseer or backra.

Gatha felt some pride in the knowledge that Poincie had "passed the worst" and that she had had a hand in it. She just wished that Poincie were closer, not way over yonder at Stokes Hall. Gatha had obtained some fabric in a bright yellow floral print and was making a dress for Poincie to be given whenever the two managed to meet again. It was a labor of love as her arthritic hands patiently sewed the garment together.

Gatha was a little surprised and somewhat amused as it was not long before Reverend Heath returned to the rectory.

"Back so soon, sar?"

"Yes, Gatha. I met a parishioner on the way and he convinced me to beat a brisk retreat back to the safety of the rectory. This storm looks to be very severe, after all."

"Then we need to board up de window and door dem, sar."

"Yes, Gatha. Two men volunteered to come and assist us with that."

The tall cumulus clouds gave way gradually to even darker nimbus as the sky began to assert its dominance. When the men arrived Gatha directed them to the back of her cottage where boards had been stowed for occasions like this. She reminded them, semi-seriously of the oft-recited folk verse about hurricanes:

"June, too soon.

July, stand by.

August, come it must.

September, remember.

October, all over!"

She was grateful for their help in boarding up her cottage as well, and offered them some thirst-quenching lemonade when they were finished with their task. They hurried home to ensure the safety of their own abodes.

Soon the rain began a steady downfall, as puffs of wind began to pelt the buildings with raindrops that moved from the vertical toward the horizontal in their trajectory as the storm progressed. This was going to be a bad storm. Gatha had seen this kind of sky before. She was relieved when Reverend Heath invited her to occupy the guest bedroom for the duration of the storm. She settled for the comfort of the drawing room couch after bringing in supplies and utensils from the outdoor kitchen.

Cudjoe raised his eyes to the sky. It was early afternoon over at the Stokes Hall Estate, but the skies were heavy, dark and foreboding. It was an ominous, premature twilight, and the curtain of cloud seemed closing fast over the sky. Stabs of lightning flashed across the sky and the thunder crashed and seemed to shake the ground. The cane fields were restless and agitated in the winds that began to increase in intensity with each passing moment. Cudjoe and other field hands had just completed their meal in the canteen when Massa Jack rode over.

"The boss says it looks like a bad storm coming! Get the great house and the Bradfords' house boarded up. Hurry! Seek shelter after that. Those with picaninnies can shelter under my cellar, some under Backra's cellar, and some under the great house. Drivers, get everybody moving! Then take shelter where you can."

Hurriedly the men nailed the prepared boards in place and headed for the cellars where they used whatever they could find to securely enclose the space for the women and children. Zinc sheets and tables were piled up to provide some shelter from the wind that was already picking up with a few raindrops pelting the workers. They had seen this kind of behavior in nature before. They knew an angry sky when they saw one. Everyone knew this was hurricane season.

Cudjoe had seen hurricanes before. There was always a time when the hurricane paused as if to gather strength to finish the work it had started. It was the calm within the storm. That would be their chance to make good their escape. He took Accompong and Johnny aside in a corner of the cellar while conversation was still possible and in the Ashanti language confided to them his plan. Johnny and Accompong were in shock.

"Say What? You mad? Dis is not a storm. Dis here is a hurricane!"

"Yes, but dat is when everybody confuse and tek shelter. No patrol, no driver with whip. Backra and everybody boarded up and 'fraid. No body looking but to save dere own skin. Dat's when we leave dis place. We run when de storm tek a breath!

Rememba de cave? The one where we hide de machete? Dat's where we hide till de next breeze. Den we go to the hills. De hurricane is we fren'!"

It was agreed that Johnny would take Little Nanny. Accompong would take a roasted breadfruit and sugar and a water canister he would steal from Backra's kitchen. They would meet at the cave, but they must not be seen to leave together. They would find their own separate ways there.

Cudjoe nodded to Johnny and tossed his head in the direction of the young massa's house. Johnny did the same to Accompong who understood that it was his job to bring Little Nanny. They would weather the storm together, just as they did the horrible Middle Passage. They were fortunate to be still together, not sold off and separated by slave auction, or the whimsy of white overseers. They were each other's good luck. They would again need good luck, especially now.

Huddled in the dark, the refugees listened to the siren whistling of the wind through the gaps in the raw, rough boards surrounding them. Soon the wind began a buffeting which shook the house and made the corrugated zinc roof and rafters creak. The raindrops pelted the roof, but soon those sounds were drowned out by the pattering on the walls as the gale grew fierce and all within the house began to feel the power of the storm. Trees swayed in the wind as their limbs groaned under the strain, and some limbs were torn from their trunks and hurled great distances as the hurricane used them as battering rams against the sides of feeble barracks and huts, obliterating them like a crazy giant gone wild. The impact of objects hurled by the wind against the boards would often surprise and terrify the refugees as they pressed together covering their heads with their arms, some praying, some cowering, some staring at the barricades, hoping they held up.

Cudjoe ventured to look through gaps in the boards and sheeting that shielded them. He saw shingles that flew like arrows off the roofs of the assistant overseer's house. Nature's fury was fully unleashed on slave and master alike, on hut and house, on humans and animals.

The sound of the rain was almost drowned out by the screaming wind and the creaks and gratings of timber under strain, punctuated by the crashing of trees succumbing to the onslaught of the elements. No one said anything. There were no doubt the screams of some but communication except by gesture was an exercise in futility. They could only huddle and hope for the storm to pass.

After what seemed like an eternity, the ferocity of the tumult began to subside and presently, they could hear the rain again. It became a steady shower and the wind subsided. Cudjoe unbarred and opened up a board and beheld what seemed like an alien planet. Every leaf on every tree was stripped bare; branches, limbs and fruit were scattered in angry disarray everywhere. The hurricane had already wreaked its havoc throughout the countryside in a tremendous, and dreadful fashion. Giant trees were sprawled across each other on the ground, and landslides rearranged the geography of hillsides. The air, water, earth, and even fire must have united in a terrible conspiracy of destruction. Bodies had been hurled across long distances, sheets of corrugated roof had sliced through trees or were now inseparably jammed into them, and small animals had been pulverized against the sides of the house on impact. Cudjoe realized the eye of the storm was passing through. It was time to make their move.

"I goin' check on dose at de big house. You all stay here. Nobody else leave. Johnny and Accompong, come wid me in case we need help up dere." He said all this loud enough for all to hear.

Nine-year-old Little Nanny insisted on going with the brothers, just as Cudjoe knew she would, clinging to Johnny's back. As soon as they left the shelter of the cellar they diverged in two directions: Johnny and Little Nanny in one, Accompong and Cudjoe in another. The devastation was extensive and the sky was still dark with rain, still blanketing the landscape as they maneuvered to their rendezvous at the cave.

Waiting longer for the storm to subside further would have increased the risk of someone coming out to survey the damage and discovering their presence. They must be well on their way when the clouds and mist cleared. The cave seemed miles away as the crow flies, but now the cane fields were flattened, affording little cover, and they had to take a circuitous route mostly on all fours to keep a low profile.

By the time the sky cleared and a swath of the blue sky appeared overhead they were only half way toward their rendezvous. They were out in the open with now clearer skies, but the landscape looked like a warzone: branches, cane leaves and stalks, uprooted trees, dead livestock, the remnants of slave huts, clothes, and to Cudjoe's horror, the body of Rufus, the driver from an adjoining estate had been flung some miles from his domicile and rudely dumped into the limbs of a tree which itself now leaned precariously.

Johnny and Little Nanny were the first to arrive at the cave. Accompong and Cudjoe took the more difficult and open route. They would fight back to back if necessary. At least Johnny and Little Nanny could stand a chance and make it. If all went well, they would wait out the second onslaught of the storm in the cave and head for the hills as soon as the storm broke. Johnny sat leaning against a large rock in the interior of the cave, looking out expectantly for Cudjoe and Accompong to arrive. Little Nanny, tired, had gone in even farther, leaning against another boulder. They waited. Cudjoe and Accompong should arrive soon.

Hoof beats in the distance. Did Cudjoe steal a horse? He had never said anything about stealing a horse. Johnny put a silencing finger to his lips and Little Nanny acknowledged the signal to be quiet. They waited as the hoof beats got louder. Johnny had never seen Cudjoe or Accompong ride a horse. This wasn't good. The cave was not a large one but Little Nanny slid in behind her boulder and was quickly out of sight. Johnny watched the entrance expectantly. He did not have long to wait.

The legs of a mule were framed by the cave entrance. And boots. Riding boots. The rider dismounted and suddenly Jack Hart confronted Johnny, pistol drawn, cocked, and pointing directly at Johnny's ample chest.

"What you doing here? You were in the cellar not so long ago! You running away? Answer me! Or I will blow a hole in your damned chest!"

Johnny, hands in the air, began stuttering a response while staring down the barrel of the gun. He was at a loss for words.

"You think I didn't see you leave the plantation? I followed you to this place. You lost me for a while but I caught up with you. Busha Bradford warned me this might happen. This time you get what you deserve, you runaway dog. This time you pay with your life. Where is the little girl that was with you?"

It is then that Little Nanny emerged from her hiding place, stepped between Johnny and Jack Hart, both hands behind her back, and blurted, "Howdi, Massa Jack."

In the second it took to collect himself and address the reality of a nine-year-old girl emerging from a cave during a lull in a hurricane, Little Nanny's hand emerged from behind her back and a stone the size of her fist reached its target between his eyes and Jack Hart fell backward, flat-on-his-back.

Johnny, equally surprised, sprang forward, grabbing the machete leaning against the entrance. He straddled Hart sideways, his knees on Hart's chest and raised the machete above his head with both arms for a clean decapitation. It was not so long ago that he had severed the arm of the poor slave whose arm was caught in the rollers at the sugar mill. This would be easier, much easier to do. The blade rose to its apex and began its descent when "Stop!" Cudjoe's shout deflected the trajectory of the blade.

Accompong picked up the pistol from where it had fallen, and Cudjoe waved Hart over to the cave entrance. He rose with fear-saucered eyes, clutching his face as blood oozed between his fingers, his nose bridge apparently broken. He was bleeding profusely. Johnny, frustrated and breathing heavily, turned around, pivoting on his heels as he let out a roar of frustration that reverberated in the inner recesses of the cave, then threw down the machete and sulked into the darkness of the cave. Little Nanny ran to his side, grabbed his stout arm and lay her head against the sweating bulge of his triceps, looking up toward his face knowingly, wordlessly. It was some time before his chest stopped heaving until he breathed a heavy sigh of resignation. He turned to address Little Nanny, rubbing her braids affectionately.

"Brave likkle girl! You save mi life. You fling dat rock like a cannon ball."

"Dem say I 'ave a mango han."

"Mango hand'?"

"Yes, me can stone a mango way up inna tree and knock it down. Me 'ave mango han.'"

He could not help but break into a laugh that dissipated his anger and returned his demeanor to something approaching normalcy. They turned to the business at hand, what to do with Hart.

"Why you stop me anyway!?" asked Johnny, still sorely vexed.

Cudjoe shook his head quizzically, as if to examine his own motive and impulse. Was it because Hart was Poincie's friend? Was it the nod of acknowledgement, a hint of respect, at the sugar mill? Cudjoe wasn't sure and didn't offer any explanation. He tied Jack's hands behind his back, tended to his wound, placed a gag in his mouth, took off his boots, and set him aside in the deepest recess of the cave. They would all ride out the storm together.

"Massa Jack. Lissen! You tell dem say the lightnin' flash, de mule bolt, and you hit you forehead 'pon a tree limb. Hear? You neva say nuttin' bout dis here cave. You hear me? And you neva see we! You understan'?"

Jack nodded. He was not about to tell George Bradford or Poincie, that he, armed, was felled by a rock-throwing nine-year-old slave girl.

The next morning when he awoke, his hands were untied, his boots were gone, the storm had passed, and the slaves were nowhere to be seen. His mule was nowhere in sight. Once again the walk-foot backra, he clutched his broken nose bridge, breathing through the mouth, and gingerly, painfully picked his way barefoot among the fallen debris and rubble, eventually reaching his humble cottage. He collapsed onto his bed, stared blankly at the main beam running the length of the ceiling and mercifully fell asleep.

CHAPTER SEVENTEEN

The Maroons

Stepping over fallen trees and debris strewn all along the bank, the runaways scanned the swollen river. No place to cross. Agitated waves of dirty brown water carrying bushes and an occasional goat, pig or even a human body, all were swept away downstream. The opposite bank was as devastated as the other. The runaways contemplated their next move. Upstream the river might be somewhat narrower, but that was closer to the next plantation and an increased risk of discovery. They would venture only so far before running into a backra, a driver, or even the militia.

Johnny hoisted Little Nanny up into a tree too slim to bear his own weight, so that she could take a look upstream.

"You see anyting?"

"No. But wait. Yes. A big tree in de river, but it don' come all the way across."

"Which side?"

"It on de odder side, but it almos' reach dis side."

"Good. We can mek a bridge."

The party skipped and jumped over fallen trees and dislodged rocks, hastening cautiously, arriving at a big tree uprooted by the ferocity of the storm. With some effort the men dragged a fallen coconut tree and standing it upright, let it fall to land between the limbs of the fallen tree. They had their bridge. It was a slow, risky business crossing over, because the two tree trunks now resulted in a make-shift dam with the water cascading over the four as they made their way with Nanny on Johnny's back, eyes closed and clinging desperately to avoid being washed away. At times a log floating downstream threatened to knock both bridge and humans downstream to oblivion.

Wet and weary, but glad to be alive, the four collapsed on the opposite bank of the river. Little Nanny looked up to Cudjoe and asked, "Many more river fe cross?"

"Ah child. Who know? But whateva we haffe do, we do. No problem."

They dared not slacken their pace though their lungs burned with exhaustion. Calloused feet, hardened by relentless hours of backbreaking labor in the cane fields, now drummed the ground in rapid cadence in a dogged stride to freedom. Accompong fared somewhat better, his feet being the only ones that could fit into the backra's boots, albeit with some difficulty. They moved quickly but with stealth, wearily but with determination. Cudjoe then had the added burden of little Nanny on his back, the brothers having taken turns carrying her when necessary, but her arms around his neck tightened his resolve. This little girl must know freedom, even if he died in securing it for her. They knew not where they were headed, but each step was one step away from the cane fields, one step closer to the hills, one step away from bondage, one step toward freedom. The mountains beckoned and they would follow.

They had heard that somewhere up in those hills was a group of runaway slaves. Others had done this; they could do it too. The ancestors would guide them. They must make the most of the darkness, the enveloping darkness that they wore like their skin: protective, warm and comforting. The morning would bring the militia when their escape was detected. They would have to find water, live off the land somehow. The Tainos had named this island Xaymaca, "land of wood and water." The land was their friend. They would keep an eye out for familiar fruit trees whether standing or fallen: cherry-melons, star apples, mangoes, and guineps that grew wild.

They reached the foothills of a great rock-faced escarpment and trained their eyes upward at the looming majesty of its elevation. The trees here had not been laid low, no doubt because of the shelter of the escarpment. They would have to scale that sheer promontory if they were ever to feel any sense of safety. The moon presently emerged from behind a cloud and the enormity of the challenge dawned on them. They would have to wait till morning after some sleep to attempt to scale the sheer cliffs of that daunting terrain. Johnny was assigned to keep watch while the others slept. They would resume at the mere hint of dawn. A few hours of sleep is all they could afford. One by one, they succumbed to restless slumber listening to the whistle of the tree frogs and the occasional hoot of a patoo or night owl. At least for the time being they were beyond the reach of the driver's lash, sleeping under the droopy eye of a half-moon.

Johnny came to with a startle. The sun was up. He roused the others and they prepared to resume their trek. Down below they could see the flattened cane fields of an estate. Their absence would have been noted before daybreak. The militia may have already been dispatched to recapture them, equipped with long poles with metal brackets that once pushed around the neck of a fleeing slave from a distance, would lock his neck in place and haul the wretch backwards to the ground and eventually back into the shackles. Later the "cat-o-nine-tails" would flail on his back and leave deep grooves and ridges that would be a constant reminder to the others of the consequences of running away.

But even as the bedraggled group came together to resume the trek, they sensed that something was amiss. It was an unidentifiable but palpable uneasiness. They fell silent and huddled together. They looked around them and then leaned their heads in varied directions, straining to hear the slightest sound that might confirm the danger they could already sense. Nothing. Only the rustle of leaves in the trees that surrounded them. Then, as if by collective peripheral perception, they sensed the trees closing in. Presently Cudjoe saw a tree move. And slowly from each surrounding tree a jonga or assegai spear emerged and then one booming voice demanded,

"A WHO UNU?"

The leaves parted and fell to the ground to reveal six Maroons armed and looking menacingly at the group. Their leader was a tall, muscular middle-aged negro with bright, slightly bulging eyes, seemingly fixed in a stare. The Maroons were dressed in woolen shirts and ragged clothes, no doubt confiscated from the plantations they had raided previously. They carried daggers, sharp machetes, Spanish swords, and water canisters of English vintage. Most of them had a jonga spear that was a stout, tall bamboo sharpened at one end to a fine point that could as easily pick a man's teeth as run him through. The leader had a flintlock pistol stuck in his waistband. He also had an assegai, a spear made from attaching a sharpened machete blade to a long bamboo or stout stick. It was Cudjoe who stepped forward.

"We Ashanti from Ghana, West Africa."

"A weh you a go?"

"To de hills, to freedom."

"Whey you cum from?"

" We come from Stokes Hall plantation."

"A wha you name?"

"Dey call me Cudjoe."

"You runnin' away?"

"Yes, bredda. Ca'an tek no mo hell."

"You come fe join de Maroon dem?"

"Yes Bredda."

"What mek you tink I believe you? You a spy, all a unu."

"No bredda. We no spy. We want be free. We wan' join the Maroon dem."

"You bring dis girl child fe mek me believe you no spy."

"No, bredda. She our likkle sista." Little Nanny clung to his waist as he pleaded for mercy.

The leader circled the group inspecting each one in turn. He was a tall muscular warrior wearing loosely fitting three-quarter pants of coarse weave and randomly decorated with splotchy stains of various hues and shapes. His shirt, what was left of it, hung from one shoulder, the other half having been torn from the shoulder and revealing a slab of chest muscle which flexed involuntarily with every gesture of his arm.

"You Cudjoe. You a driver at Stokes Hall?"

"No Bredda. Me jus' cut cane."

"Mek me see you hand dem." The leader inspected Cudjoe's outstretched hands feeling the calluses while the other Maroons kept their weapons raised, poised for anything untoward. Satisfied that Cudjoe spoke truly, he moved on to Accompong.

" Wha you name?"

"Accompong."

"Wha you do pon the plantation?"

"Me carry cut cane from de field to de sugar house, and me roll de barrel dem full wid rum pon de cart dem fe carry de rum pon de boat."

He stopped at Johnny. "And you. Wha dem call you?"

"Johnny."

"Johnny? Dat not African name. Dat is English name, spy name."

"No Bredda."

"So what you real name?"

"Me name Jonga, but dem call me Johnny." The leader allowed a half smile.

"Jonga, like dis?" He raised a weapon.

"Yes."

"Wha you do a' Stokes Hall?"

"Me de axe man in de sugar house. When de cane feeder get dem arm inna de roller dem, me chop off de arm."

The leader circled Johnny who did not move, looking straight ahead. The leader seemed to sense that here was a man with physical attributes and temperament similar to his own. He stood behind Johnny and then without warning grasped his tunic at the neck and ripped it from top to bottom. Johnny still didn't move. His back fully exposed to the air was a spectacle to behold. It was a conglomeration of welts and scars of pock-marked undulations and the raised scar tissue of many an overseer's lash. His back resembled the rugged Jamaican landscape around them. Some wounds were still festering and oozing pus mixed with blood.

"Me see dat backra mek you back raw. Dis ya back look like de hills afta de hurricane." He nodded and the warriors lowered their weapons. The leader faced Johnny, pursed his mouth with a mere hint of a smile and nodded, as if to say we are men, you and I.

Dis likkle girl pickney would be good fe de village. Plenty boy but no enuf girl pickney. Dis one don' say much. Him keep quiet. But dis one like chat- chat. Me spirit no tek to him, dis one name Cudjoe. Could be trouble. But dis big one could be a good warrior.

*When me is chief dis one coulda be a fighta.
Maybe dem not spy. De chief can decide. Me
bring dem to him. Him will decide.*

In the end, Cudjoe was convinced that
Little Nanny's pleading eyes and Johnny's
pock-marked back tilted the scales in their
favor.

"Mi name is Vasco. You don' need 'fraid
of we. Come. We mus climb dis here
mountain. It dangerous dung here. We mus
move quick-quick."

He beckoned them onward toward the
mountain. From the thicket they trudged
through the bush until they intercepted a
footpath, a winding trail of red soil amid the
greenery of the brush and the rugged
outcroppings of limestone that flanked the
path. Some of these outcroppings were high
enough to be grasped to heave oneself up to
another level of the path as they negotiated
the steep ascent. At one particularly rugged
stage Vasco paused and retrieved from his
tunic an abeng, a cow's horn with a hole at
the tip of the pointed end and another
bored along the side a few inches from the
pointed end. He brought it to his mouth,
directed the flare toward the escarpment,
and using his thumb at the small hole at
the end to control the rhythm and tone,
blew a staccato signal, then waited. The far
away response came within seconds, the
same staccato rhythm. A half smile briefly

graced his face. He nodded to the others and the party trudged on.

Vasco disclosed that his party had been tracking the refugees for some time. He had first noticed a clump of Shamey Macca plants, folding ferns, and knew that someone had passed that way and the general direction of travel. He showed the runaways a clump of Shamey ferns looking perfectly normal but when touched the leaves instantaneously folded in on themselves as if ashamed. After a few minutes the ferns would gradually unfold, revealing how long ago they had been disturbed. The ferns were like plant spies in league with the Maroons.

The leader volunteered that the settlement they were heading toward was one of many on the island, from the hills of St. Thomas to the parish of Trelawny. There was one village called Me-No-Sen-Yu-No-Come, a warning to the Spanish militia and later the English: " If I don't send (for you), you don't come." Another was called The Land of Look Behind because the Spanish soldiers knew that they were in mortal danger when they ventured into that territory, so two rode on each horse, one soldier seated the normal way, and another sitting facing backwards to look behind for the inevitable Maroon ambush.

The party paused briefly to refresh themselves at the Stony River. They filled two calabash gourds the Maroons had brought and splashed water over their faces and bodies. Above them loomed the sheer escarpment which seemed to deny any human access, but that is where the leader indicated by a wave of his hand they would be going. It was easy to see that any soldiers attempting to breach that natural fortress would face a daunting task, and the resistance above would have the advantage of gravity accelerating the velocity of rocks hurled from above. Of the rocks there would be an abundant supply of every size and shape.

A large cotton tree loomed ahead, and here the group paused. There seemed nowhere to go from there. The path seemed to peter out and eventually merge with the bush behind which was a sheer rock face, high and unscalable without a ladder and ropes. Behind the tree was a cliff falling hundreds of feet down to a honeycomb of jagged rocks that would make mincemeat of any falling body. Below, the weathered bones of at least three skeletons lay in gruesome disarray, scattered among the pockmarked limestone formations where John Crow vultures had picked them clean.

"We climb de tree," the leader ordered, and one Maroon scaled the giant limbs and seemed to disappear into the tree. When the refugees followed suit they discovered that the tree had a hollowed out trunk, a shaft reaching to its base. They emerged from between its buttress roots to discover a breathtaking vista. And for the first time they felt safe and free. Before them was an undulating terrain robed in greenery, a spreading panorama of hillocks interspersed with narrow valleys, a rugged but beautiful landscape which spelled freedom. The rain had served to enhance the greenery of the landscape and only the summits of hills showed the ravages of the hurricane. They began the ascent of a narrow series of steps carved into the mountainside, made even more hazardous by the recent rains associated with the hurricane.

It was already noon and the sun bore down fiercely from a clear blue sky, but they had far to go. Already they had encountered another Maroon party going in the opposite direction to take their place below the escarpment. The party crossed a small stream showing weathered and bleached rocks on which no doubt women did their washing, then proceeded as the path grew even more steep as they proceeded toward the summit of the hillock. Finally, a plateau unfolded as they breached the summit.

Beneath a canopy of poinciana trees they saw the village. They advanced along a broad promenade of flat open ground smoothed and hardened by countless footsteps. On each side there were clusters of huts and lean-to's on the ground swept clean with brush brooms. Unlike the square huts at Stokes Hall plantation, these were round with dome-shaped roofs neatly grass-thatched. Each had an open doorway, the entire structure supported by a framework of wattle.

At the far end of the dirt promenade was a large overhang of rock as to form a cave with a gaping mouth and shade where scores of Maroons were at work on various tasks cleaning up after the hurricane. Some huts were obviously damaged but not to the level of devastation evident down below the escarpment. Despite some hurricane damage, it seemed for all intents like a well-organized African village.

There were children running around, some naked, some clothed, all barefoot. After the cleanup effort they played ring games and bows and arrows and seemed to enjoy themselves without being boisterous, no doubt a security measure to safeguard their location. One small boy approached Little Nanny, introduced himself as Scipio, broke a naseberry in two pieces and offered her the larger. She graciously, wordlessly, accepted and began to feel the warmth of a home.

The little group of refugees was ushered toward the overhanging rock and into the large high-ceilinged cavern in the middle of which a large pot was cooking on a fire made of logs and three large stones on which the pot stood. Between the stones was the firewood being stoked by a woman and a young girl, both squatting low on the ground, perfectly comfortable in that posture. Large limestone projections hung from the ceiling of the cave and pointed to their counterparts on the ground. On some of these sat Maroons of various ages, though those on these stalagmites were older, the younger ones content to sit on the ground. Some reclined on animal skins spread on the ground while others sat on the wood stumps from fallen trees.

There was a particularly large stone rising up from the floor of the cave and set back away from the boiling pot. On this sat the Chief, a beam of light streaming down where he sat. When Cudjoe looked up he saw that there was an opening in the roof of the cave and between the branches and green leaves of a bush he could see the blue sky. There was the Chief, his black skin glistening in the golden beams of the sun filtered by the greenery of the bushes high above him. The blackness, greenery, and gold sunbeams seemed somehow comforting.

"A who unu?"

"Dem run way from de Stokes Hall Estate Chief." It was Vasco who answered.

"My name is Cudjoe. Nuff respek to you, Chief."

"An' who dese?"

"Dis is Accompong, and dis is Johnny. Dem both me brodda, Chief.

"And who dis likkle one?"

"Di girl pickney name Little Nanny."

"Nanny? Dat is a big name for a likkle girl. In Africa only a woman of honour have a name like dat."

"Well, Chief. She likkle but she born before de time; couldn' wait to be free. An' when she come out de womb her madda said she had a vision dat dis child would be a great woman, a priestess in de tribe. We call her Little Nanny from dat day. Den the medicine man start teach her tings, and herbs, and the wise sayings of de elders."

The Chief continued interrogating the refugees, conferred with Vasco who stood next to the chief, and assigned a Maroon to teach them the rules and regulations of the village he governed like any African village that this group of runaways may have come from. Finally, he addressed the crowd gathered to inspect the newcomers: "Some of we is Ashanti like me an dese. Some Coromanti, some Ibo, some Mandingo, and some in dis village is Taino and some mix of all kinda blood. We live here as free people! We is one people out of many! Maroon foreva!" "Maroon foreva!" the crowd echoed his words and surrounded the newcomers, welcoming them.

The morning after their arrival at the Maroon village, the chief summoned the new arrivals. Cudjoe, Johnny, Accompong and Little Nanny gathered round after their breakfast and the clean-up detail.

"Come, mek we tek a walk." He spoke in characteristically subdued tones, like a father to his children. They ambled along into the bush as he deftly used his assegai as a pointer and walking aid and, as they all knew, when necessary he could use it as a deadly weapon.

"De lan' is our fren.' Modda Naycher is our guide here jus like in Africa. We nuh rape and use de lan like the white man. We respek Modda Eart'. She on our side and she protek we. Now, de fus ting is livin in de bush. An de fus ting you need is wata. Try fe know weh de riva dem deh. Stay close to de riva if you can."

"But what if we not near a riva?" Little Nanny wanted to know.

"Dats when we use cacoon. Come ova ya." The chief beckoned them over to a thicket and with a deft slash of his assegai severed a cacoon stick. He held the neatly slashed end over his mouth and drank a steady drip of water.

"Now, food all ova de place if you know weh fe look. We eat thatch-head and mek susu soup. We call it thatch-head; dem call it heart of palm. We peel it and eat de food inside. Den we find de makola grub worm and we eat dem. Everyting raw. Maroon no eat salt. When de English come fe fight we, we eat uncook food. We no cook wid open fire 'cause dem will know weh we deh. Only when de mountain cover wid mist and fog we cook outside."

Accompong wanted to know what meat Maroons ate.

"Hog, man. Wild hog. We hunt dem down an cook dem wid pepper an spice. We cook dem in a hole we dig in de grung. We cover de meat wid all-spice wood and it cook long an' slow. We call it jerk. De Taino people show we how fe dweet. One ting you must learn quick is how fe hunt hog."

The chief waved his hand above his head as though to shoo away a pesky fly. It took Cudjoe a second look to see that it was a gesture in response to a signal from a scout high up in a tree, that all was well. Presently they came to a grassy clearing in the jungle.

"Dis is de Asafo Ground. Is here we have gadderins an' dis is de trainin grung fe fightin." Some thirty young warriors were being instructed in the art of foliage camouflage. Here the chief got a mischievous glint in his eye as if to share a private joke.

"De English try fe find we and ambush we wid dem soljas. But we smaat! We use de bush fe fool dem, so dem no know dat when dem see tree and bush is really we dem a see. Dat is how we ambush dem---wid bush."

The recruits had a lively chuckle with Little Nanny's giggle delighting the chief who took a liking to her like the grand daughter he never had. The chief pointed them toward a small group of warriors that were being bushed. First a suit of cacoon vines had been prepared and carefully wrapped around the torso of each warrior while songs and incantations were vocalized. Then the shrubbery was ceremonially fixed in place. Cudjoe and the others watched as from head to toe every inch of the warrior was covered. Not even the eyes were visible. Warriors took turns covering each other's bodies, especially their backs. Older warriors completed the task with considerably more speed, while ensuring freedom of movement of arms and legs and concealment of weapons such as jongas and long guns.

"Tomorrow unu mus come here an start dis. Learn it good."

Over in a corner of the Asafo ground was a small group of warriors being trained in the use of the jonga. Their instructor looked back at the newly arrived party and they instantly recognized Vasco, the tall scout leader who initially met them below the escarpment and guided them to the Maroon settlement. Cudjoe's face beamed with recognition and he waved at Vasco. The latter's response was unexpected. Vasco stared coldly. He looked away and resumed his instruction. Cudjoe looked at Johnny who happened to notice the exchange and both looked quizzically at each other.

Cudjoe would be careful after that. He must find out what went on in Vasco's mind. Was it resentment? Jealousy? Was the chief showing Cudjoe or the others any favoritism? Or was there something deeper than that? From the marks on his cheek Cudjoe recognizd the markings of the Ibo tribe. Was that it? Did the Ashantis sell some Ibos into slavery? Cudjoe decided that the chief's personal interest in them was the reason for the ugly looks. It was jealousy, since Vasco didn't seem to have the same reaction when they met below the escarpment. Suspicion then, yes. Resentment, now. But why?

PART TWO

CHAPTER EIGHTEEN

A Hog Hunt

The supply of hog meat had been quite adequate for weeks, the jerk pork lasting a long time because of preservative herbs and spices and the methods of storage. But that supply was running low. It was time for another hog hunt. The hunting party was led by Cudjoe and Nanny. Accompong accompanied them and four others, all armed with jongas or assegais, a few knives and machetes. It was to be a long expedition lasting days as necessary, so they carried crocus bags with supplies slung over their shoulders. These bags were also needed to carry the meat back to the village. With the party were two veterans of these hunts, the mongrel dogs, Sticka and Jooka. Vasco was left behind, it being generally understood that he relished fighting but had no liking for cultivating crops or hunting wild hogs. Those duties were better left for those so inclined.

The Maroon chief had seen the young Cudjoe as a warrior who had the mark of nobility. His African ancestry and family had cultivated leadership and a fierce regard for freedom and a love of the land. The chief announced to the village that Cudjoe would assume the leadership when the time came. Now, some years later, with the old chief gone to his eternal rest in the realm of shadows, Cudjoe had taken control of this and many other Maroon villages on the Leeward side of the island. Then he and Nanny had travelled to the windward side and established ties with the settlements there. It would take many villages to win a war with the English. Cudjoe knew this. Nanny, now a young woman with wisdom far beyond her years, was the guiding force behind their undertakings. She had proven her bravery and fierce love of freedom through many hunts and raids and was renown for herbal healings as well as a formidable warrior and leader.

The hunting party left in the cool of the hours before daybreak silently following a footpath that led through the Asafo Ground and beyond. Sticka and Jooka trotted along with lively gait, seemingly as excited at the prospect of another adventure in the wild. When the footpath ended they pressed on into the jungle where they were forced to make their own way, using their machetes to hack through the thick underbrush as they went.

By sunrise they had negotiated their way through the rugged terrain into the rolling hills and emerged from the bush into a grass covered hillside where they could scan the green vista of a rugged but vibrant geography basking in the brilliance of the morning sun. There was a refreshing sense of freedom here. This was far away from any plantation, any estate, any threat to their well-being. Not even Maroon patrols would be found here. Their trek took them miles away from any other humans, closer to the territory of the wild boar, the king of this Jamaican jungle.

From their hillside they looked across to the next ridge and down to the narrow pass where both ridges converged. They assumed there was a stream because of the clusters of bamboo strewn in a hodge-podge manner on either side of the pass. Nanny seemed able to summon the hogs with a low guttural grunt, funneling the sound through her circled palm and raising her head toward the rising terrain of the ridge across from them. They had descended a few feet when the dogs began to whimper, both leaning forward anxiously on their legs and pointing their noses to the other side of the mountain, their eyes fixed on the opposite slope. Cudjoe urged the others on, skipping down the hillside now, and the dogs were already ahead of them racing through the thick grass, occasionally leaping over the greenery, charging toward the stream.

Nanny followed not far behind, nimbly accommodating the undulating, uneven ground almost as adroitly as Sticka and Jooka. Suddenly the dogs stopped. Still whimpering with excitement they paced back and forth, swishing their tails, confused. They looked at the hunters, perplexed. Nanny explained that they must have descended below the scent. She sensed the bewilderment, but she knew the scent must have originated high up from the opposing ridge. It was a quiet morning, no discernible breeze.

By then it was well past noon and the party reached the narrow stream, quenched their thirst, and replenished their gourds of water. Soon the sun and the sweat of their exertion would require the water they carried and more. Sticka and Jooka lapped from the stream and then Cudjoe, with a sweep of his hand, beckoned them upward toward the summit of the ridge. Now the hunters were on greater alert. Above them the grassland continued, but the trees and shrubbery thickened the closer they looked at the summit.

They had trekked one hundred yards up the side of the ridge when they heard the urgent, agitated barking of the dogs somewhere in the thick of the jungle. The hunters hastened in that direction, hacking away the vines and brush, the lower limbs of the trees that formed a dark and shadowy canopy. They moved in the direction of the barking and as it grew louder they divided into two groups, Cudjoe and two others, and Nanny and three hunters including Accompong. They would separate and converge from opposite sides of the suspected location of the wild hog. They would corral him toward each other with the hope that one of their jongas would find its mark. Now the barking became frantic. The two dogs were obviously engaged in a desperate encounter. They must hasten to their aid.

Soon there was a shout from Nanny. "Him a come!" The men could scarce see each other in the shaded underbrush but Cudjoe caught a fleeting shadow of an enormous beast that charged through the underbrush with such ferocity as to leave a hole through which the dogs gave chase. The party, now reunited, followed as best they could. Presently they came upon a partial clearing where they saw Sticka and Jooka engaged with a boar, perhaps the largest that Cudjoe or Nanny had ever seen. They had cornered him against the moss-covered trunk of a giant fallen tree. His back against the tree trunk, the boar was slashing back and forth with his tusks as Sticka and Jooka deftly skipped out of reach, but only barely. The taunting barking of the dogs, the shouting of the hunters, and the deep, guttural gruntings of the hog made a raucous commotion that seemed to shake the very leaves of the trees and bushes.

From the side Cudjoe observed the beast. It was some five feet from head to rump with a trashy, stringy tail that flashed to and fro as he thrashed about. It could easily outweigh two of his warriors combined. Its overall color was a dirty yellow that turned more to orange as the eye scanned from the belly to the top of the ridge forming the spine. The sides were worn smooth like wrinkly leather, but straggly stretches of coarse orange hair ran along the spine and under the belly. The line from the rump to the back of the beast became a raised mound of flesh that rounded the shoulders and sloped into the neck bearing an enormous head covered in coarse, straggly hair which seemed permanently fixed to stand on end.

Just then Sticka leaped at the boar's neck. The brute swiveled aside as tusks slashed in response, ripping a long streak of open flesh in her side. The wound opened to spill the intestines of the dog whose bark became a shriek of pain as she landed in silence, her chest rising and falling rapidly as she panted frantically. She lay on her side, her insides on the ground beside her.

The beast turned and looked in Cudjoe's direction. It seemed to sense that Cudjoe was the leader of this intrusion on its territory. But it was Jooka who confronted the beast, challenging it head to head, snarls and grunts competing in ferocity. The hunters, jongas poised to lunge at the first opportunity, hesitated. The dog would be impaled easily on a mistimed thrust. With one dog immobilized they were about to bring an end to the matter when the hog launched Jooka flying over his back with a quick upward jerk of its head. Now the beast was angry. It lowered its head and charged toward Cudjoe as jongas swooshed from all sides, most missing their mark. Nanny lunged forward, her jonga hurtling though the air, but the missile was deflected as the moving target pounded forward in full tilt, all its bulk fully engaged. It refused to be dispatched by these intruders.

Cudjoe, his jonga raised and ready, took a step back to affirm his footing. It was an unfortunate circumstance. His heel caught on the raised roots of a nearby tree and he fell flat on his back, still clutching the jonga. He raised his head to see the massive head of the beast, two short but pointy ears atop squinty eyes and a long, flat, hairy, rugged face atop a long snout with flattened end from which two nostrils pointed outward to the sides. The jaws curved upwards in a cruel smile at the ends of which two sharp tusks emerged on either side of the jaw. The lower jaw line, recessed under the overhanging snout, boasted two substantial tusks, larger than those above, emerging from the front of the jaw and extending upward a hand's width above the snout.

Cudjoe knew the boar would aim for his groin. Instinctively, he raised the jonga upward at the very last instant when the animal lunged. The jonga disintegrated as the animal impaled itself and collapsed in a heap, partially crushing him under its bulk. The hunters thankfully rolled the animal off him, as he wiped the foul-smelling blood from his chest and belly. The hunters danced and whooped and then turned quickly to where Sticka still lay, her chest still heaving. Jooka stood near, licking her face.

Nanny and one of the hunters knelt beside the dog. He reached for a small pouch from which he extricated a large needle and some coarse thread wrapped around a short dried stick. The others watched as he washed the laceration, examined the entrails, and carefully repacked the cavity. Then he employed the needle and thread, closing up the wound. Then Nanny applied a poultice of chewed herbs that she had prepared in the meanwhile. She held the poultice in place by crude strips of cloth torn from her shirt. The rest was left to Mother Nature. Sticka would rest in a crocus bag carried by the hunter until she died or reached the village.

Meanwhile, the afternoon shadows lengthened into evening and the hunters prepared to spend the night. But first they needed a fire, and one hunter gathered the kindling and logs from dead trees nearby and with flint succeeded in creating a roaring fire while others prepared to butcher the hog. Someone brought out the yams, cho-cho, dasheen, and cocoa they had brought, along with scotch bonnet peppers and many herbs and spices which one hunter had brought in a big pot of English manufacture.

The ground provisions were washed or simply brushed clean, their skins intact, and cut into bite-sized chunks with machetes. Broad, flat flour dumplings the size of a man's palm were thrown into the pot that chortled, bubbled, and gurgled in a most pleasing way as it sat supported by three large stones with burning wood arranged between.

The entrails of the hog having been removed, a piece of liver was set aside as an offering to the ancestors. Nanny performed a brief ceremony in acknowledgement of their presence. A Maroon removed the tusks of the boar, cleaned them, and with a stringy vine made a crude necklace. He approached Cudjoe and prostrated himself, holding up the necklace in submissive fashion. The others crossed their jongas across their chests. Cudjoe acknowledged their gesture, bowing and lifting the necklace high above his head, reciting the names of his ancestors as he danced round and around. One hunter used a stick and drummed on the hollowed trunk of a dead tree and soon the others joined in the dance in sheer euphoria that lasted for quite some time.

The animal was quartered and portions kept in crocus bags for transport, but not before choice portions were skewered and placed on a spit over the fire for their feast that night. The hunters used broad leaves and calabashes to hold the ground provisions along with spicy, lick-you-finger roast hog. They relaxed around the fire, sharing stories of times back in Africa, the torturous Middle Passage and their escape to freedom as Maroons. They were in high spirits, sharing Anancy stories and jokes well into the night until they fell asleep around the fire, one person keeping watch as they slept. At the first rosy blush of dawn they began the return journey.

Their homecoming was a cause for celebration. The villagers welcomed them back as heroes. They had fulfilled their task and proved they were worthy of responsibility for the well-being of the village. Cudjoe had shown himself a brave leader and Nanny clearly emerged as a leader in her own right. The village celebrated long into the night. The drums rang out into the jungle night as the campfire blazed and chanting and dancing continued around the fire.

A portion of the hog was roasted over the fire while some Maroons cut the rest into pieces and prepared the herbs and spices needed to do a proper "jerk" that could be stored for many weeks after it was slow-cooked in ground cavities. It was good to be alive and free. The hunters recounted to eager ears the encounter between Cudjoe and the wild boar. The Maroons were jubilant and Cudjoe's bravery and cool composure under threat of death endeared him to them all the more. All were in a jovial spirit except for one Vasco, who lurked in surly solitude on the fringes of the group. He retired to his hut before most of the others. From the periphery of his line of sight Cudjoe watched the shadowy figure as it slunk away into the darkness.

CHAPTER NINETEEN

The Drums of War

Cudjoe heard the faint but distinctive staccato of the abeng. That rhythm indicated intrusion from the west. He had long awaited this signal. He had known that raids on the Stokes Hall Estate and others nearby would sooner or later elicit a military response. Indeed, he had been hoping to trigger that reaction. It was 1690 and his time had come. The south was too great a prospect for a regiment, the way he and his brothers and Nanny had come when they escaped and confronted the escarpment. The militia had elected to take the western approach, trudging through the unforgiving, undulating terrain. The militia was on its way, but he was ready.

The old chief had groomed him well for leadership: "Don't fight de white man in de white man way. Mek him come to you. Mek him fight you on you own grung. Force him fe fight Maroon on Maroon terms. Foolish white man dem line up dem army facing each other on a open space. Then dey open fire on each odder, kill a whole heap of soljas on both sides till a few leave standing on one side fe claim the vicktry. De white man have no respek for de land, de earth, and not even for de lives of dey own soljas."

No, Cudjoe would fight to repel the English army while minimizing the danger for each precious Maroon. He would fight them guerilla-style with the earth as an ally. They would have to fight both the Maroons and Mother Nature at the same time.

The subsequent daring raids on the armory at Stokes Hall and two other plantations netted the Maroons the ire of the governor and nettled his resolve to track down the pestilential Maroons once and for all. Cudjoe would not let these English dictate the fight. The inevitable confrontation was at hand, but they were more equipped to fight than ever before. Cudjoe would make the governor regret that decision to punish the Maroons for their brazen defiance, and the disgrace the militia had suffered variously at their hand. Speed and surprise would overcome numbers and equipment. "So dey tink o'we like stupid animals in de bush? Good. Let dem no expek much from we. Den we surprise dem de more."

But one thing was bothersome. A unit of scouts led by Vasco, had been assigned to patrol below the escarpment. They returned without him. He had told them that he had been given a special assignment and would not be returning with them. Cudjoe had not given Vasco any special assignment. It had been two weeks since Vasco had disappeared. This could mean only one thing. Vasco had become a deserter. And Vasco knew too much about Maroon warfare, habits, and secrets. Vasco had become a threat to their very existence.

The prospect of war rested heavily on Cudjoe's mind. Last night the brave warriors, young and old, had rested peacefully in their huts, made love to their women, cuddled their young ones to sleep. By tonight some could return with grievous wounds to never fight again, and some could lie stiff and cold on the rugged terrain of the landscape they now called home. Women and children would wail the loss of their men, fathers, and brothers. Cudjoe could well be among the dead. Then what would be the fate of those left behind?

Nanny had suggested they build a separate village, deeper into the interior, where women and children could be relocated when a war became inevitable as now. That would be a matter to be undertaken when the present crisis was past. For their part, the women were as anxious to defend the village as the men. Cudjoe would not deny them that privilege.

He would let the English get as far as Macca Ridge. By then they would be tired from the heat and would be suffering dehydration, their water canisters well-nigh empty since they wouldn't have the benefit of the Stony River. Stupid English soldiers would be wearing full uniform, walking heat chambers and sweat boxes all, easily seen in their red uniforms and with white sashes criss-crossing their chests, perfect target crosshairs for Maroon sharpshooters. And the Maroons were well-trained sharpshooters. Cudjoe had used the seized muskets and ammunition to good advantage, cautioning the warriors not to waste a single shot. Make every discharge count. When their ammunition ran out there would be the bows and arrows, then asseguis and jongas. Even the children and Nanny, now a young woman, had been trained to use the bow and arrows tipped with poison. They all knew how to use the assegai and the jonga.

At Macca Ridge the soldiers would have to proceed in single file. There was no other way up the ridge to the plateau above. His men would be ready.

Presently a young Maroon came running, assegai in hand, toward Cudjoe as the faint sound of an abeng wafted on the breeze. This was a southern signal. The English were converging on two fronts? The Maroon reported that there was a large regiment of

English soldiers approaching from the west, nearly 500 strong. This was more than was anticipated. The cross–island militia must have been mobilized. Cudjoe, Nanny, Johnny, and Accompong converged in a huddle to decide how to contend with this new development. Nanny had wisdom far in excess of her years, listening and interjecting as necessary. Cudjoe often deferred to her counsel.

"Dey tink we so busy defendin' from the west dat we doan notice dem comin' from the sout'. Right?"

"No man. But dey tink we no watch the sout' because of the high rock face. Dey tink we tink dat dey no able to come up the rock face so we defen' from de west while dey come up over the rock."

"But dem cyan' come up from the sout over the rock!"

"Dat's what dem want we fi t'ink! Dis is de work of Vasco. Dis is how Vasco brain work. Dem have sailors who used to climbing rope ladder and swing from rope and use claw to board ship when dem pirating. Dem can do it!"

"So, we haffe defen' from two front. West and sout'."

"Yah man! Nanny and Johnny, you will tell all de wimen and picaninnies to collek rock stones, big and small, and stack dem near the edge of the rock face. Then tek the ashes and twenty young warriors. You know what to do. Accompong, you an' me work the West side. "

Before the warriors were deployed, Cudjoe called the entire village together in the central clearance before the cave. As he emerged from the shadow of the overhanging rock with Nanny at his side, he addressed them:

"Now look here broddas and sistas! De massas and backras and soljas all band together and dey comin' to attack we. Dey tink because dey rich and have more tings dey betta dan we. De powerful weaka dan dey look, and we stronga dan we look. Dey tink dey strong but we goin' to Anancy dem! We ready long time fe dem. We practice with gun, bow and arrow, jonga, assegai, machete, and rock stone. We ready! But is not jus we. We bound to win becuz we and de land is fightin' for the same t'ing: freedom! De land been rape and mash up to line the pocket of the English. The scars on me back testify to the cruelty of de English and all of you have de same experience. So we not 'fraid to fight. Dey have fifty to we one, but one of we equal to one hundred a dem, and we have de land on our side and the African ancestas will guide us. Nanny already talk to dem. Dey is with us! We cannot fail! Mek de English come! Me machete thirsty, me jonga hungry, me arrow anxious, me rock stone heavy and me musket ready fe belch! Mek dem come!"

At this the men and women raised their hands high above their heads and the very leaves on the trees rustled with the sound of their cheers as the children leaped off their feet and joined the chant of " Me no sen, you no come! If you come, you no go!" and ever louder "ME NO SEN, YOU NO COME. IF YOU COME, YOU NO GO!"

By this time three young Maroons with their drums had taken position just inside the cave and the latter was like an echo chamber reverberating the hypnotic rhythms as they drummed, one alternating the heel of his hands with his collective fingers on the animal skin membrane of the drum, another keeping the beat vigorously with the sides of his hands and with a single finger stroking the drum from edge to center to produce a deeply felt moaning sound. The third maintained a syncopated cross beat which jolted the listeners into shivers of movement and a body-thrilling dance that was impossible to resist. Everyone, men, women and children were caught up into a paroxysm of movement until the hard earth trembled with the rhythm. ME NO SEN, YOU NO COME! IF YOU COME, YOU NO GO!

Their shouts reverberated in the echo chambers of the cave and out into the trees where they mingled with the breeze and wafted down the escarpment and stirred the curtains of the Stokes Hall Great House in the lush parish of St. Thomas. They rattled the glass windows of the Governor's mansion in Port Royal and rustled the sails of the ships in the harbor. It was a gusty, restless breeze.

CHAPTER TWENTY

The First Maroon War

George Bradford steadied his bulk by reaching out to the walls on either side of the narrow alley as he navigated his way with unsteady steps from the Cat and Fiddle toward the rooming house where he stayed on his trips to Port Royal. The alley was unlit save for a naked flickering torch extending from its sconce on a wall behind him, so the alley darkened as he made his way forward. As he neared the edge of the structure his way was blocked by a dark figure impeding his progress.

"Outta my way!"

"Yes Massa, but a minute of you time, please."

"I don't know you. Outta my way."

"But I know you Massa Bradford from Stokes Hall."

"What do you want?"

"To help you, Massa."

"I'm not drunk."

"I don' mean dat kinda help Massa."

"Why would I need your help?"

"Me know tings dat you don't know."

"And who are you?"

"Vasco, Massa. Massa, you lose some slave some time back when the breeze-blow come and mash up tings on dis island."

"That happened on many plantations and this happened some years ago. Tell me something I don't already know."

"De slave dem you lose was Cudjoe, Johnny, Accompong an a likkle girl name Nanny."

"How come you know that....What you say your name was?"

"Vasco, Massa."

"What you know about these escaped slaves?"

"Dey turn Maroon. Me was Maroon."

"So you escaped from what estate?"

"Hampton Estate, Massa."

"Why are you telling me all this?"

"Me can lead you to dem. Me know where dey hide and me know how fe get dere. Me can help you hunt dem."

"So what do you get from all this? What do you want?"

"Mek me a free man."

"A free man." Bradford found that amusing.

"An' gimme a hundred pound."

"A hundred pounds? What makes you think you have information worth all this?"

" Me was wid de Maroon dem. Me know how dem live an how dem fight. Me can help you, Massa. Massa fren dem will respek him when dem see him gi dem the viktry."

Bradford looked closely at his face. Though the alley was dark, the moon was in its third quarter and as Vasco turned Bradford saw three horizontal scarred slash marks on his cheek. Hmmm....I bet he would claim to be the son of a chief.

" Interesting proposition, Vasco. How can I meet you again to discuss this?"

Vasco hesitated as visions of militia with muskets aimed at his head flashed through his mind. He had seen the capture and torture of runaways. He had been lucky so far. He cannot trust this white man. After all, one of the governors, in pretense of peace, had invited a group of Maroons to eat with the governor on one of His Majesty's ships. When they were all assembled in the banquet hall awaiting the governor's arrival, the ship sailed away and the Maroons were never heard from again. Vasco must not take any chances.

"When you comin' back to Port Royal Massa?"

"In a fortnight."

"I will look for you, Massa."

"Very well. I will talk to the colonel about this and let you know what's what."

"Tenk you, Massa. I will fin' you when you come back."

Vasco was about to take his leave but hesitated. "One more ting, Massa. You rememba long time now 'bout de white man who get kill on Spanish Town Road?"

"You mean Justice Swaby?"

"Same one."

"Well, me know who kill him."

"A Maroon?"

"No. De Maroon dem have a fren name Kwaku. Him hide in the bush since Swaby got kill and some of dem tink is him do it."

"Where is this Kwaku?"

"Him have a donkey an' him sell food to people at de house dem and sometime in de market here in Port Royal."

"Thank you, Vasco. I will see you in two weeks." Hmm...That fella bringing food stuffs to Stokes Hall on his donkey. Never did get the name. Could that be Kwaku? If he ever saw that son of a whore there again....

The men of the cross-island militia felt somewhat optimistic about the outcome of the operation they had undertaken. Never before had they been amassed in these numbers and there was safety in numbers. Many overseers, backras, and even some planters had joined with the regular militia. Besides, the fortunate circumstance of George Bradford's genius in convincing a Maroon deserter to be their guide in locating and fighting the Maroons was additional reason to be confident of victory. George Bradford had seized the opportunity to earn respect and broaden his network of European acquaintances.

Bradford assigned Jack Hart to remain behind, since one of them should always be at Stokes Hall to keep an eye on things. Bradford felt quite competent in handling a flintlock pistol and musket. Besides, he had a score to settle with those runaways. It was a festering boil in his chest and it must be lacerated. He would not tolerate their impudence. He could then inform Lord Stokes of his exploits in revenging the loss of these and other slaves by tales of his bravery against these rebellious Maroons. They would pay, so help me God!

The Maroons had been successful in minor skirmishes and raids on local plantations, but this would be a force to be reckoned with and Bradford was a part of it. The English seemed ready to "get down to brass tacks" on the Maroon issue. The Maroons had helped the English to harass and finally drive out the Spaniards, but broken promises had created a rift between the two parties and now the Maroons had become a weed that must be uprooted.

Vasco was near the front of the assemblage, Bradford beside him, as they navigated the bush, the shrubbery, the thickets, the trees. He swung with his machete at the overhanging brush and vines, the low-hanging limbs of trees, clearing the way for the men following behind, feeling a new sense of importance. They eventually approached the escarpment and Vasco could be seen pointing upward to the sheer rock face, gesturing in explanation of how it could be breached, The men of the cross-island militia followed him eagerly. Bradford patted him on the shoulder and nodded approval. The force split into two companies for the double frontal assault from different directions, a smaller group remaining just below the escarpment while the larger force maneuvered westward.

Vasco had brought them as far as he could. He retired to the back of the assemblage, stashed the English clothing he had been given in the fork of a tree, and melted into the bush. The rest was up to them. It was a strange circumstance that had brought him to this awkward situation. But what else could he do? He remembered looking at the small circle of warriors, the Maroon council of elders. Nanny, though a grown young woman, was the youngest, and the chief the oldest and now quite frail, but alert and still full of wisdom. Then there was Vasco, and Cudjoe was the fourth. They were gathered under the shade of a tree on the edges of the Asafo Ground. What would they do when the English attacked? Their raids had nettled the English army enough to guarantee repercussions. It was not a matter of if, but when the attack would occur. Vasco thought they should reduce the numbers of English who could mount an attack:

"Mek we pison de wata. De tank and wata barrel dem."

"Dat will kill woman and child too. We no have no danger from woman and child. Ongle soljas." Cudjoe disagreed.

"And de slave dem drink from de same tank and barrel," Nanny enjoined.

"Cudjoe and Nanny talk troot. We no haffe kill pickney and woman dem," the Chief chimed in.

"Anyting me want, unu no want." Vasco was quite displeased. Ever since he brought these newcomers to the village the chief seemed to side with them. He remembered the days when he and the chief made all the decisions for the village. Now, too many opinions made decisions harder. Back in the African village his father, the chief, gave orders and no one argued, and especially not a woman. This young woman Nanny didn't know her place.

Nanny's suggestion that they make a special camp for women and children was particularly unwelcome:

"De woman dem who want fe fight can fight, but the pickneys and moddas shoulda have a place dem can hide so if we get kill, dey can carry on de Maroon life afta we gone. We shoulda mek a special camp fe dem inna cave."

"But we need evry one of dem woman fe fight, even the packney dem. Me say everybody fe fight."

"Nanny mek sense, but mek we talk bout dat later." The chief had more pressing things on his mind it seemed. It was becoming clearer with each meeting: Vasco was not as favored as before. The chief clearly favored Cudjoe as the new chief when he was gone. Vasco's best chance was after the chief had died. Then he would make his move. When the English scattered the Maroons, who else would they have to turn to? Who could rally them together and train them to fight another day?

The soldiers' day-long march had brought them to progressively rugged countryside. Officers had left their horses at a base camp as the terrain became more the domain of mountain goats than humans and horses. Soon their phalanxes were abandoned in favor of single-file columns, since this was the only way of coping with the narrow footpaths winding among the limestone formations that honeycombed the terrain. It was a perilous path on narrow ridges and between sharp outcrops that could tear a uniform and rip the skin. Silently, in the trees and in the crevices of the rocks the Maroons waited. Each Maroon was competent in "bushing up," attaching foliage to their bodies to so resemble shrubs and bushes that a soldier could be standing next to the warrior with no idea of his mortal danger. On a nearby ridge Accompong and his men trained their sights on the rear of the column where one man, after attempting to be the backward lookout realized the futility of his task since forward walking was itself fraught with peril.

As the last man passed, the limestone came alive ever so stealthily. The rocks seemed to move as Cudjoe and his men, ash-covered, closed in behind the adversary. Then, like a mass choir, one collective shout broke the silence, startling the soldiers, and one immediately fell over the side of a cliff as, startled, he lost his footing. A staccato sound of musket fire started from the adjoining ridge courtesy of Accompong and his warriors and men began to fall at the back of the column and progressively toward the front. By the time those in front, disconcerted by the sudden shouting and gunfire, regained composure, they found it necessary to turn around to face the direction of fire, losing precious seconds as the gun fire continued, cutting them down, so that they tumbled to the mercilessly sharp rocks below. They realized there was no retreat and no advance.

Their scarlet uniforms, criss-crossed with white sashes across their chests made them visible, easy targets under the dark shadowy canopy of the trees and bush. No sooner was the ripping sound of leaves pierced by pellets than there was sudden impact and it was all over. Militia were falling in rapid succession, no time to reload after ill-aimed muskets made feeble attempts at resistance. Red coats fell thick as leaves in an autumn storm.

Accompong and the other warriors in the trees descended to join Cudjoe's band as together they went slashing, thrusting, stabbing, and pushing red coats off the ridge before they could reload their muskets. Many of the soldiers in the front of the company fled to the cover of the trees in less perilous terrain and took cover behind the larges trees forming a canopy overshadowing the undergrowth of high grass and shrubbery. This was exactly what Cudjoe had anticipated. Many a red coat took cover behind a tree, bush, or shrub as they desperately recharged muskets to offer resistance.

Cudjoe watched from behind a tree as from many a shrub a machete or dagger promptly emerged and slit throat of a red coat. He had trained them well. Soon there was return fire from the remaining English soldiers. Cudjoe peered from behind the tree, saw a puff of smoke, heard the discharge as a lead ball plunged into his right shoulder, causing a searing pain. He grabbed his shoulder and retreated behind the tree trunk, gritting his teeth. He looked again, quickly. He saw his assailant's head retreat behind the trunk of a large tree.

He knew his own musket was not readied for discharge. Neither was his assailant's. Patience he told himself. Patience. He reloaded with some difficulty, propping his gun between his knees while he recharged using his left hand. There was enough gunpowder for only one good shot. The red coat's fire had come from the right hand side of the tree trunk.

Sooner or later, the red coat would stick his head out from the left side. It was something the old chief had taught him. Cudjoe aimed for the left side at the height of the soldier's head. He ignored the throbbing pain in his right shoulder, the spasmodic but incessant gunfire and shouting around him, the whoops of delight from fellow Maroons as lead balls found their mark, the cries of the vanquished. Patience. He waited, left finger on the trigger, breath held, arm steadied on the side of the smaller tree trunk behind which he had taken cover. He waited. Soon a head emerged, a finger flexed, a musket belched, and a face disintegrated as the well-aimed blast found its mark. Cudjoe's smile was intercepted by a grimace as he grabbed his wounded shoulder.

Soon there was an eerie silence, save for the moans of English fighters writhing in pain from assegai wounds and ripped flesh.

Dead soldiers lay like a grove of fallen coconut trees after the ravages of a hurricane. A unit of Maroon warriors nimbly negotiated the crevices and crannies of the ridge, salvaging the corpses of the soldiers, collecting the spoils of war: muskets, pistols, water canisters, swords, bayonets, ammunition mostly unused, uniforms, boots and belts, personal effects such as rings and crucifixes, even eyeglasses. Soldiers still alive were dispatched with a single swish of a machete, stab of an assegai, or thrust of a jonga. No use wasting ammunition. The John Crows hovering overhead waited their turn to feast on fresh carrion. They would have a banquet lasting for weeks.

Meanwhile, Cudjoe and most of his warriors hastened to the escarpment where Nanny, Johnny, and some handpicked young men plus the women were holding out against a smaller force of militia. They needn't have bothered. A force of seventy-five had encamped at the base of the sheer rock face and began using grappling hooks to scale the sheer verticality of the promontory. They were about half way up the rock face and preparing to throw their hooks up to the edge of the massive cliff when rocks rained down with deadly accuracy on their heads, and soldiers above fell with deadly impact on those below as they plummeted to a common destination.

Women and even children, used to stoning mangoes high up in trees with deadly accuracy, employed their acumen with telling results. "Mango hands" don't miss! And English heads are bigger than mangoes even if sometimes their brains seemed to approximate that size.

From above came gunfire as Cudjoe and his warriors joined in the melee, lying flat on their bellies and picking off soldiers with deadly accuracy. At the first sign of retreat the warriors descended to the base of the escarpment via the large cotton tree and pursued the soldiers killing all but one as Cudjoe had ordered. The two others at the base camp with the horses had long gone, only too glad to be alive. They would almost certainly become pirates since the governor would assume they had suffered the same fate as their compatriots, and their desertion would no doubt mean that they would swing from Gallows Point in Port Royal.

It was an ignominious defeat. Now it was time to send a message to the Governor. Cudjoe, Nanny, Accompong, and Johnny knew what that meant. It was the Maroon way. One fighter had been wounded but not fatally. His pistol had been confiscated before he could blow his own brains out.

Cudjoe nodded to Johnny to do the honours. The procedure was simple: George Bradford was stripped naked, his pale, bulbous hulk bound to a large tree trunk at the ankles, under the ballooning belly, under the armpits and the neck. Then his body was methodically caressed with the branches and leaves of "Cow Itch," a most potent cousin of the poison ivy family. Every square inch of his frontal anatomy and any available orifice was subject to this herbal therapy. Johnny was slow, systematic, and meticulous in discharging his duty.

Welts, red and bulging, began to emerge all over the backra's skin. Soon the welts spread and joined to give a red, overall puffy appearance as low guttural moans and grunts were punctuated only by the need to catch a breath between agonized writhings. They spared the soles of his feet. Thus, his body was on fire without the luxury of immolation. When George Bradford seemed about to give up the ghost he was set free to find his way back to his superiors and to tell his tale of woe to the English governor, Sir Thomas Modyford. The Maroons had defeated a vastly greater number of soldiers of the English army.

CHAPTER TWENTY-ONE

The Morning After

Now, after the first Maroon War, Vasco faced a dilemma. What could he do? He couldn't return to being a slave. Bradford had promised him freedom if he helped the English win against the Maroons, but they had lost the war. In any case, the English didn't always keep their promises. With this loss, they may even use him as a scapegoat, claim that he led them into an ambush. Could he return to being a Maroon? He was a man without a people. The whole thing started when Cudjoe and the others joined the Maroons. And to think that Vasco himself had brought them up the escarpment into Maroon country. He should have run them through with a jonga the first time he met them. Soon after the arrival of Cudjoe and his group, the chief started giving them special attention, treated them like royalty. Vasco was a prince back in his village before he was captured and sold to a slaver. Not fair.

Vasco should be the leader of these Maroons, not Cudjoe. The only chance he had would be to challenge Cudjoe man-to-man for the leadership. He brought Cudjoe in, and he could take Cudjoe out! When he killed him he would explain how he gave the Maroons the victory by bringing the English to the Maroons so the Maroons could defeat them. He is the one who forced Cudjoe to fight the English because Cudjoe did not want to fight. Vasco was the true hero of this war. Vasco was the weapons trainer for the Maroons. He could fight and beat anybody. No one could match his skills with any weapon. Of that he had no doubt. If necessary, he would become leader by mortal combat.

Cudjoe had been wounded and Nanny set to work that same night digging out the lead ball with a bamboo stick. She used a poultice of herbs and wild honey to draw out any infection, bound up his shoulder wound, and immobilized the arm with a sling fashioned from vines. On this, the morning after the first Maroon war, Cudjoe, carrying his trusty assegai, left the village early and alone and went deeper into the jungle to the Asafo ground to pay respects and give thanks to the ancestors.

The jungle was quiet save for the distant crowing of a wild rooster. He returned taking another footpath that went past the village toward the escarpment. But somehow he had the distinct sensation of being watched. He walked on. Then from the corner of his eye he saw a flash of sunlight from among the greenery. It was the familiar glint of a blade reflected by the sun. The war was fought yesterday. No need for warriors to be bushed up and carrying a weapon today. Was he being stalked? By a Maroon? Keep walking. The hair on the back of the neck seemed to stand up while a chill flashed upward like a cold breeze from the base of the skull. Cudjoe swirled around to confront the watcher. At first he scanned the thinning shrubbery and trees before focusing on a thicket seemingly out in a clearing, a characteristically unlikely place for such a growth.

"A who you? Wha you want?"

The figure threw off the shroud of leaves and foliage to reveal a tall muscular negro, assegai in hand. The blade glinted blindingly in the sunlight.

"Vasco. You a traita to yu people."

"No mo traita dan yu people in Africa who sell fe me people. Dat is why we end up in dis place."

"We no inna Africa now. You neva notice?"

"Tek me from me people but you ca'an tek me people from outta me."

"So you show de English weh we deh. You show dem how fe come ya. You tell dem fe attack we from two direction. You plan neva work."

"You no see dat me bring dem to you? You beat dem 'cause me bring dem."

"You tink me fool? Dem mus a promise you someting. You lef we an come back wid de English fe kill we. Why you hate we?"

"Me a Maroon. Me no hate Maroon. Me hate you."

"Wha me do to you?"

"You tek me place ya. From you come ya de chief no pay me no mind. Me was chief son in Africa. Me a de true leada fe de Maroon afta de chief dead. Everybody know dat. Till you come ya."

"De chief choose me ova you. Is my fault dat?"

"No. Is my fault. Is me bring you ya. An me tek you outta ya."

Clearly angry, Vasco advanced in combat stance, assegai in hand. A warrior descended from his scouting elevation in the trees, and others began to converge as an abeng summoned them. They converged on the clearing, jongas and assegais in hand, some carrying machetes, some bows and arrows, all readied for the moment when Vasco made his move. Nanny jumped between Cudjoe and the adversary, her assegai twirling from hand to hand.

"Cudloe. Yessiday you fight like lion. Now you have only one arm fe fight wid. You no haffe prove nutn'. No mek him draw you inna fight. We know you is de leada. You give we big viktry yessiday. Mek me deal wid him."

Johnny joined Nanny, forming a human shield, daring Vasco to attack their leader. Sticka and Jooka were agitated too and whimpering, straining forward, ready to charge at Vasco. They had to be restrained by Accompong who was ready to release them at the next threatening step forward. By now the entire village seemed to have converged on the pair. Cudjoe waved them all back as he advanced to within striking distance. The morning sun bathed their dark, muscular torsos and bedecked them both in fire. Vasco smiled a bitter smile. Cudjoe fixed Vasco in his gaze.

"Dis is betwixt me an you. You want be chief. Den you haffe kill me first."

"You pay respek to de ancestas. You do de right ting dis marnin. You goin' join dem soon. You know you ca'an beat me. And a one-arm man can neva beat me. You forget dat me teach you all you know 'bout fightin?"

"You teach me good, Vasco. But jonga, assegai, and machete is not everything, you son of a she-goat!"

Vasco sneered, his lips quivered, and the veins on the side of his neck bulged. The glow of the morning sun on his dark, oiled skin underscored the fierce contours of his face in high relief. He lunged forward.

Cudjoe raised his left arm as the blade flashed between torso and arm, touching neither. Clearly the taller of the two, Vasco pressed his cause, slashing, swirling, driving, stabbing, jabbing, plunging, every move potentially deadly. The blade, sharpened white, flashed its cruel smile at every thrust. Cudjoe stepped back, parried, feinted, deflected, fended off, dodged and side stepped. Vasco was undeterred. The onslaught continued. Vasco pressed forward. Cudjoe backed up.

Each man tried to use to his advantage the few trees near the escarpment. Dodging a thrust, Cudjoe narrowly sidestepped just before grabbing the shaft of Vasco's assegai, holding it against a tree trunk, he being on the opposite side of the tree. There was a monentary pause as Vasco reached for his machete and in a flash swung the blade at Cudjoe's head. The head snapped back but not enough to avoid the slash that appeared on Cudjoe's cheek, first as a white streak which then turned red and dripped blood. The machete lodged deep into the tree trunk, defying all attempts to dislodge it. A collective gasp rose from the crowd and the dogs began a frantic barking. Cudjoe fought back. Flashes of light reflected on the stabbing blades of desperate assegais. The villagers stood with twitching hands, their heads craned forward, eyes fixed in a horrified stare that begrudged the luxury of a single blink.

The crowd parted to give them room as they approached the edge of the escarpment. Cudjoe glanced from side to side, aware of the sheer chasm and the distant trees in the valley below and behind him. Vasco is left-handed. Circle to the right. He is angry, but not enough to lose his temper. Anancy say, " Mad dog no have time fe see snake."

"You ca'an do more dan dat, Vasco? You mumma mus did open har leg dem fe a wart hog!"

Vasco bristled. His eyes flashed fire. His countenance darkened by two shades. The fingers tightened around the shaft of the assegai. He crouched, his weight resting back on one leg, the other extended as his knee trembled uncontrollably. Vasco charged forward, hurling himself at the enemy. It was the weapon that went over first as Cudjoe ducked, extending a leg, and as the assegai disappeared over the edge of the escarpment Vasco momentarily arrested his own momentum, flailing his arms, and hovered but for a moment before tripping over the outstretched leg and took a header, plunging with flailing arms and legs into the abyss.

The villagers, open-mouthed, heard a distant thud from below just before they let out a collective breath of relief. They rushed to the edge to look down to where they had sent so many rocks flying onto English heads the day before. A crumpled clot of human flesh lay mangled on the rocks.

CHAPTER TWENTY-TWO

Lord Stokes

Lord Stokes rose from the burgundy wing chair he had been sitting in and walked over to the semicircular alcove at the far end of his private study. He looked down from his second-story vantage point and surveyed the expansive manicured lawns, sculpted hedges, the lily ponds, and the weather-beaten sculptures that were evenly spaced along the long graveled driveway leading up to the front entrance of his mansion. It was a rare sunny day in his rural borough in England. The driveway stretched from the graveled grand entrance all the way to the roadway where it met an ornate iron gate which from that distance was reminiscent of the setting of an exotic ring enclosing a massive diamond, except in this case the diamond was substituted by a crimson crest bearing a stylized "S" rendered in gold.

Lord Stokes threw open one of eight tall windows of beveled glass set in diagonal patterns and let in the fresh air. That was when he noticed the mail delivery boy departing down the driveway where an attendant let him out through the gate. Soon there was a polite knock at the door. He turned to face the mahogany door, both his hands clasped behind his back, and drew himself to full height as the door opened.

"Yes."

"A letter for you, my lord, from the West Indies."

"What Island?"

"Jamaica, my lord."

"Read it to me, Mrs. Bertram."

"Yes, my lord." She reached into her bosom and retrieved a pair of ancient reading glasses, the kind with just the lower half of lenses. Using an arm of the glasses as a letter opener, she opened the envelope and installed the spectacles onto her face and ears. Adjusting back and forth the distance from face to paper, she settled on a distance of perhaps six inches and began to read:

Robert Long to Lord Stokes, Montego Bay, Jamaica, January 21, 1692

My Dear Lord,

Many developments having transpired since my last missive to my Lord, I find it prudent that I apprise my Lord of certain matters of interest to my Lord and to the continued financial buoyancy of the holdings here in Jamaica.

As my Lord is aware, the estate at Stokes Hall had suffered substantial damage from the hurricanes that devastated much of the island. While the great house withstood the storms commendably, it had suffered some relatively minor damage, mostly to its roof, but having been built like a fortress by Lord Luke Stokes it emerged in good shape, and repairs have all been completed.

The overseer's house, occupied currently by George Bradford and his wife, was however, not so fortunate, and neither was the cottage occupied by his assistant Jack Hart. These have required more extensive repair. Some of the sugar cane crops fell victim to hurricanes that flattened the fields and resulted in a net loss that was partially absorbed by our reserves, but the losses were substantial. These fields were promptly replanted to salvage what remained of the growing season.

While there are these setbacks, there are also developments presenting opportunities for my Lord to increase his acreage and expand his potential for a greater return on his investment. Proprietors at Amity Hall and Hampton Court indicate their willingness to surrender substantial acreages so as to mobilize capital needed to ensure the viability of their estates. If my Lord could with our help negotiate these acquisitions, the long-term benefits could be substantial. These proprietors, however, would require your presence to assure them of the seriousness of our intentions. Let me suggest a visit as soon as feasible to take advantage of this opportunity. We would be happy to make all the arrangements for your visit as we have before.

Believe me to be, my dear Lord,
Sincerely yours,
Robert Long
Attorney at Law

Mrs. Smith, having read the letter, peered over the half lenses, her wrinkly eyes capped by the scraggly remnants of greying eyebrows.

"Thank you, Mrs. Smith. Leave the letter on the sideboard."

Lord Stokes returned to the alcove and looked out on his estate once more, but his mind was lost in a reverie. For his part he did not particularly relish the obligation of a visit to Jamaica. That was a negative prospect because his father, Lord Luke Stokes, had left his governorship of the tiny West Indian island of Nevis and with him some one thousand, six hundred settlers, servants, and slaves, and resettled in Jamaica. Unfortunately, the older Lord Stokes fell prey to the epidemic of yellow fever that also decimated most of his entourage. Lord Stokes, Lady Stokes, and most of the children were all dead within a span of two months. Lord Luke Stokes had gone from being a big fish in a very small pond to a guppy in a toxic aquarium.

Nevertheless, all was not lost. He had bequeathed multiple properties to his remaining children of whom the young Stokes was the eldest remaining, thus inheriting the title of his father and his holdings. Stokes Hall Estate was his to have, to hold, and to exploit in support of his lavish lifestyle in a borough in rural England. Mrs. Maud Bertram, her own husband also having died of yellow fever, was the matronly relic of his early days in Jamaica, a remnant of the household that he remembered before tragedy struck. An English servant of his father's, he had brought her back to England to supervise the staff and servants of his English estate.

His Jamaican estate was quite suitable for a man of his station and he remembered the Stokes Hall great house before tragedy struck and brought his father's dreams of glory to an end. On the whole, he would have preferred to enjoy his English lifestyle without having to visit Jamaica and be exposed to the savagery and degradation of human beings on this sugar plantation that made it all possible. Would not one lose one's appetite if every time one were presented with a cooked steak, one would have to first witness the corralling, stabbing, plaintive bellowing, dying, and ultimate dismemberment of a cow?

The Stokes Hall Great House of his youth was an imposing structure. It was built as much like a fortress as a house with gun holes strategically placed in its walls. The two-story house consisted of three hip-roofed interconnected towers, the kitchen as a separate structure, and a water tank. The house was made of concreted rock rubble-faced with dressed stone or a stucco coating in some areas. There was some fancy arch work on the outside windows and doors, the lintels being of timber. The long driveway leading up to the main entrance was flanked by rows of slave quarters hidden behind rows of trees and hedging. Below the great house at a respectable distance were the overseer's house and a smaller structure, an assistant's cottage, both slightly elevated on a mound and separated from the slave quarters. Other buildings on the property were barns, warehouses and sheds dedicated to the production of sugar and rum for export.

On the day of his arrival, as arranged by Solicitor Robert Long and his law firm, an ornate four-wheeled carriage with four horses awaited him at dockside, as did John White, president of the Colonial Council and Reverend Emanuel Heath who had been a personal acquaintance of his father's.

After a brief stop at the appropriate government offices to register his august presence he was on his way to St. Thomas and Stokes Hall, all this carefully orchestrated and facilitated by Robert Long and his staff. An armed escort of eight militiamen accompanied him on his journey that would take the greater part of the day. His arrival at Stokes Hall in the early evening was pleasant, the temperate climate being quite agreeable in comparison to his chilly English air even this early in June.

As the carriage entered the long driveway between two stout columns supporting the ornate iron gates, he began to recall his early childhood days on the estate. Some of the trees had been replaced by younger saplings not yet at full maturity, and the slave quarters having thus been more openly exposed were to his mind too obvious at the moment. However, as he approached the great house he was pleased to see the servants all lined up in two phalanxes on either side of the main entrance and in unison executing an obviously well-rehearsed curtsy. George Bradford was there, and Mrs. Bradford, and so was Jack Hart.

For most of those gathered to welcome Lord Stokes, he appeared younger than they had envisioned. As he exited his carriage they saw a slim, pale-faced young man in his late twenties, with understated facial features, wearing a long dark coat and a light green waistcoat showing brass buttons, light-colored breeches, and a patterned neck kerchief tastefully covering his neck and throat.

Lord Stokes was back in his Jamaican home, but not for long. He intended to spend the greater part of his time in Spanish Town and Port Royal where he hoped to reorganize his Jamaica holdings to maximize his financial returns, and in between all this to enjoy the life of leisure for which the island, especially Port Royal, was famous. What is more is that Robert Long had presented to him the gilt-edged and embossed invitation that had been sent to various members of the Jamaican aristocracy and plantocracy:

The pleasure of your company is requested
at a ball
in celebration of the visit of

Lord Stokes

At the Governor's Mansion, Port Royal
Friday, June 6, 1692 at 8:00 p.m.
until time indeterminate

RSVP

As he savored the prospect of this social indulgence, his fevered imagination, fanned by the fires of youthful desire, had suddenly unshackled him from the conventions of polite decorum to which his personage was, by virtue of his station, obliged to observe back in his English domicile. Stokes knew that he could rely on the discretion of his peers on the island because he recalled that as a child he had often heard the elders say, "Port Royal keeps her own deepest secrets, and she buries them deep." It was a truism he would soon come to know for himself.

CHAPTER TWENTY-THREE

Reunion

Ever since Reverend Heath had arranged for Poincie to have some time off from Stokes Hall to visit himself and Gatha in Port Royal, she had been eagerly anticipating the visit and preparing for it. She had learned to knit and crochet as Mrs. Bradford had offered to teach her, and had knitted a woolen sweater for the reverend and crocheted a set of lacy white doilies for Aunt Gatha's little center table in the little cottage behind the rectory.

When the day came for her departure from Stokes Hall, she having done everything she needed to do for Lord Stokes' visit as directed by Mrs. Bradford, packed a little "grip" with her essentials and some changes of clothing and donned her best walking shoes because this was to be an arduous journey. Stokes Hall was relatively close to the main road, so she set out early to catch a stagecoach that would carry her toward Kingston, and change to another that would take her to Port Royal.

The stagecoach was a two-horse affair with a driver elevated on a ledge in front from where he manipulated the reins of the horses and could look out for any highwaymen who often held up and robbed these vehicles. The coach itself could accommodate four passengers inside but an additional two would sometimes sit beside the driver. Behind the cab a guard would sit protecting the original purpose of the coach: the transport of letters between various government posts along a prescribed route. These letters were housed in a large box boldly carrying the words Royal Mail. At each stop the box would be opened to leave letters for that post and accept new letters.

Poincie was relieved when she saw an approaching two-horse coach behind her and paused by the side of the road to signal her need for a ride. She was even more grateful when, upon climbing aboard she found a vacant seat in the cab with an old white man who looked drowsy and was soon asleep, his head rocking against the wood frame of the window with each bump on the road.

The ride was harsh and bone-jarring because the road was bumpy and the stagecoach had no springs, but every bump was a little closer to Port Royal. Sometimes when a coach was full of passengers the driver, on approaching a steep hill, would stop and let the passengers go on foot until they reached the crest of the hill so as to spare the horses. After what seemed like many hours involving passengers departing and embarking and a change of horses, she boarded another stagecoach for the last leg of the journey to Port Royal. Not long after, it stopped at government offices on Queen Street where Poincie left for the rectory on foot, her "grip" in hand.

It was late afternoon as she approached the rectory, and she had the fascination of seeing again the familiar and yet half–forgotten features of the front yard: its meandering path, the rose bushes, the polished front door and the step...the step where she was told her crude cradle had been placed shortly after she was born. She paused and pondered the significance of that spot and the gratitude she felt for the two wonderful human beings even now on the other side of that door. Her knock was firm and answered by Reverend Heath himself who gathered her to himself like the long-lost daughter that she had become, and when he finally released her he shouted to Gatha.

"Gatha! Come here this minute!"

"What sar? Something wrong sar?"

"Come look and see who is here!"

Gatha entered and on seeing Poincie she virtually ran the last few steps to hug and rock her from side to side, stopping to look at her face, then hug and rock her again in a dance Reverend Heath had never seen before but enjoyed watching.

"But putoos, yu lookin' good! Prettier dan eva!"

"Yu lookin' good too, Aunt Gatha!" Reverend Heath stood by with a broad smile, savoring the reunion. The years had been kind to him. He had the same kind face and had become respectably portly as was typical of a man just approaching the twilight years. He then excused himself, since he had promised to meet with John White at the Blue Anchor for a drink that evening.

The two women commiserated long past midnight, laughing at old times and comparing notes of experiences each had had while away from each other. "Kwaku say everybody at Stokes Hall luv yu," Gatha informed her. Finally, it was time to get much needed sleep. When at last Poincie readied herself for bed, Gatha informed her that Reverend Heath had insisted that she occupy the guest room at the rectory for the duration of her visit. As they both entered the room, Poincie saw on the bed a beautiful yellow dress that Gatha had lovingly made for her. "Try it on darlin'" Gatha said, and Poincie complied, twirling round and round for full effect. The dress fit perfectly. Poincie slept blissfully that night.

The next morning, Poincie arose early and joined Gatha in preparing breakfast which they and Reverend Heath enjoyed together in the dining room on its oval table, the polished mahogany still gleaming with regular polishing thanks to Gatha. They enjoyed boiled green bananas and roasted breadfruit along with ackee and saltfish, plus pawpaw slices, and Johnnie cakes for good measure. Reverend Heath topped this off with English green tea while Poincie and Gatha were happy with their cocoa. "Yu been de joy of me life, darlin'" Gatha told Poincie sipping on her hot cocoa. "You and Reverend Heath mothered and fathered me. Thank you both. I can never repay you."

Later that morning, Kwaku, having had contact with Poincie at Stokes Hall and knowing of this visit, came by on his rounds and stayed with them for a while. Gatha had suspected he would visit and saved some breakfast for him, which he enjoyed immensely and as always was not shy in expressing his appreciation for Gatha's kindness.

The three relaxed under the shade of an ackee tree in the backyard, Reverend Heath having left for St. Paul's. Soon Gatha left the two young people talking as she tended to her duties inside. Kwaku turned to Poincie and said,

"Poincie, I think it's time you know everyting 'bout me."

"Look. I don't push you because I know you helpin' the Maroons and some tings you mus keep to yuself."

"Yes, but it is more dan dat."

"You have a terrible disease?"

"No."

"You have a woman up in de hills?"

"No."

"You have pickney wid baby modda?"

"No."

"You like man more dan woman?"

"No."

"You kill anybody?"

"No."

"Then me no have fe know anyting more. Me already know dat you no rich."

Just then Gatha rejoined them and they enjoyed each other's company some more, both ladies entertained by Kwaku's many stories until it was time for him to take his leave with the faithful Calypso. It was then that Poincie heard a loud knock on the front door and went to investigate, leaving Kwaku and Gatha in the backyard. Apparently not satisfied with the promptness of the response to the knocking, there was no one at the front door when she opened it, but she heard a disturbance at the back of the house. She ran there only to see three militiamen arrest and restrain Kwaku who was loudly protesting as they tied his hands behind him. Gatha was loudly pleading as to the cause of this intrusion but the men ignored her.

Poincie barred their exit through the side gate, demanding an explanation. One was emptying the contents of Calypso's hampers into a large, official-looking bag, and in response to Kwaku's question of what they were doing with his goods one replied curtly, "evidence." "Evidence of what?" demanded Poincie. "Murder," was the reply. Then Poincie and Gatha were roughly herded out of the way as the men took Kwaku away in what looked like a crude paddy wagon drawn by a single horse.

The two women were very troubled as they contemplated what could happen next. Freedmen were known to disappear or if granted a trial could be subject to heinous consequences. Gibbetting (hanging) was known to be the punishment meted out for murder. Kwaku had just told her that he never killed anyone. They would have to inquire as to where he was held, quite likely Marshalsea prison, and inform Reverend Heath of the unexpected turn of events. Poincie dared not distress Gatha with the dark fear that this might be about much more than about Kwaku, that in some way she may be implicated. Had the authorities discovered Kwaku's role in the acquisition of weaponry for the recent Maroon War? Could they have also discovered her role? Was she next?

Poincie tried to banish these thoughts from her mind, but said nothing to Gatha, nor indeed to Reverend Heath who not long afterwards returned home. When he greeted them he instantly recognized their distress and Poincie quite animatedly explained the afternoon's developments and pleaded for his help. Heath promised to make inquiries as to where Kwaku was confined and added, "I will contact the solicitors from Montego Bay. They will be in Spanish Town tomorrow for a meeting at the council chambers. Kwaku will need a lawyer if he is to get any measure of justice. Oh, and by the way, let Calypso graze in the backyard. The grass is getting high and needs cropping anyway."

Chapter Twenty-Four

Kwaku on Trial

Kwaku was transported from Marshalsea Prison in Port Royal to the court in Spanish Town for trial on the charge of murder. On the appointed day, he was ushered into the court in the main square of the capital where he met and consulted with Robert Long, a defense lawyer whom he had never met, provided for him through the efforts of Reverend Heath and his connections with the law firm in Montego Bay, the same firm entrusted with the stewardship of the Stokes Estate.

The court was housed in an imposing government office building rather than a separate courthouse as was the case in Port Royal. The Spanish had erected the complex on one side of the main square in Spanish Town with their characteristic colonnades and arches, all done in red brick. When the English took control of the island they applied plaster to the façade of the building and finished the exterior surface with fine rendering.

The court had a full docket that day, and there was standing room only, the bleachers all full, the seats on the main floor occupied by the well-to-do. There was a balustrade separating the crowd and the official territory of the staff, lawyers, and the accused as well as the witness stand, and all was resplendent in polished mahogany. The entire chamber was elaborately constructed with both crown and base molding. Elevated above the entire ground floor was the judge's station with a backdrop of polished mahogany and carvings of official English insignia.

The Bailiff, with the required solemnity, and with an obvious sense of his own importance, entered the courtroom and raised his voice loudly enough to be heard above the din of the crowd. The courtroom was already sweltering from an oppressive heat that would intensify as the day progressed. "Hear ye! Hear ye! This court will come to order, presided over by Justice William Beeston on this Monday the Second day of June in the Year of our Lord One thousand, sixteen hundred and ninety two! All rise!"

The assembled rose in their seats, and those in the bleachers already on their feet promptly observed silence as his Honour Judge William Beeston entered and sat on his elevated platform. He was a pale, gaunt man with drawn face framed by the appropriate judiciary straw-colored wig covering his presumably bald head. He had squinty eyes that seemed constantly to peer through the small round lenses of his spectacles poised precariously on the edge of his nose. The spectacles were of rather thin, wiry construction that often seemed to be indistinguishable from the irregular grid-work of wrinkles on his face.

"Kwaku Johnson, there being no statute of limitations on murder, you are here charged with the crime of murder, an offense committed on Sunday, the 23rd of February, 1682. It is alleged that at approximately 7:00 o'clock of that morning along the Spanish Town Road you in cold blood bludgeoned to death Justice of the Peace Archibald Swaby. How do you plead?"

"Nat guilty, Yurranna!"

"Let the record show that the accused pleads 'not guilty.' The prosecution may proceed."

"Kwaku Johnson, what do you do for a living?"

"Me sell yam and dasheen and cocoa, and baddoe and yampie and paw paw and punkin and banana and mango, and guinep and starapple and june plum and cho-cho, and...."

"That is enough. We understand! Now where do you get these things to sell?"

"Me 'ave a likkle cultivation in St Thomas an me grow likkle a dis an' likkle a dat, all kinda tings fe sell. Den when me no 'ave enuf from me cultivation, me go a de slave grounds an' me buy the extra dem 'ave, fe serb me customa dem."

"Customers? You have customers?"

"Yes sar. It easier fe me go a de house dem an supply de people, so dem no 'ave fe go to market so offen."

"Then if your cultivation doesn't have enough ground provisions and the slaves don't have any extra to sell you from their garden plots, where do you get your food stuffs?"

"Dat neva happen sar. Dere is always supm fe sell. Sometime more, sometime less."

"Mr. Johnson, you are a freedman?"

"Yes, sar."

"You have proof of that?"

"Objection!" Defense counsel rose to his feet.

"State your objection," Judge Beeston responded.

"Your Honour, Kwaku Johnson has been a freedman well known to most people in Port Royal and elsewhere for these past several years as he has gone door-to-door selling his foodstuffs. His freedman status is not the issue here, and has no bearing on his guilt or innocence. That question is not germane to this case."

"Sustained. I would encourage you, counselor, to confine yourself to the details of this case. We do not have time to waste here. We have a full docket. Please continue."

The prosecution called its first witness of the day: Mary Carleton. Kwaku was visibly surprised to see her, whom he considered a friend, as a witness for the prosecution. He looked at Robert Long who proffered no consolation, seeming to be just as perplexed. This woman could be dangerous. True, Long could attack her credibility as a prostitute, but she knew the well-to-do and in the most intimate ways. She would be handled with kid gloves by both sides. She knew too much about too many influential people in too many compromising ways. After she took her place in the witness box and was duly sworn, the prosecutor proceeded with the examination.

"Miss Carleton, please state your occupation."

"I operate a tavern and a gentleman's lounge." At this there was a noticeable murmur of amusement at the euphemism for a whorehouse that Miss Carleton had been widely known to operate.

"Miss Carleton, has the accused Kwaku Johnson done business with your establishment?"

"Yes sir."

"Objection! The question is ambiguous Your Honour, meant to sully the reputation of my client."

"Counselor, please rephrase your question."

"Miss Carleton, what has been the nature of your business with the accused?"

"I have bought ground provisions from the accused. It saved me many a trip to the open-air market."

"So you were a client of his, but he was not a client of yours?"

"That is correct, counselor."

"Miss Carleton, just how well do you know the defendant? Have you ever seen him anywhere else but at your establishment?"

Mary Carleton hesitated, looked down as she perfunctorily straightened her dress and straightened up, minding her posture, clearly disturbed by the question posed to her. "Well, I recall.... I happened to see him once away from my place in Port Royal....just in passing."

"Yes? Where exactly did you see him?"

Mary Carleton was visibly torn, wrung her hands, turned her head from side to side as if to rearrange the contents of her troubled mind.

"Please answer the question, Miss Carleton."

"Pardon me, Your Honour, but I just took an oath to tell the truth, and the truth is...."

"Yes? Go on."

"I saw him once along the Spanish Town road."

"That is a long road Miss Carleton. Be more specific," the prosecutor suggested.

"Near the big cotton tree beside the Spanish Town road, counselor."

"So, was he walking or riding his donkey at the time?"

"Counselor, the first time I saw the accused he was riding a horse...."

"Kwaku Johnson was riding a horse, not a donkey? How could a common laborer ride a horse, Miss Carleton, unless perhaps he stole it?"

Mary Carleton seemed reluctant to respond.

"Objection. Leading the witness, Your Honour!"

"Sustained."

"I will rephrase the question, Your Honour. Miss Carleton, how do you explain Kwaku Johnson, a common laborer, riding a horse along the Spanish Town road?"

"That man, Your Honour, that man is not Kwaku Johnson. That man is John Bolt!"

The prosecutor seemed outraged. "Madam, are you insane? John Bolt has been the original prime suspect in the death of Justice of the Peace Swaby. Bolt has been missing for years. You are obviously mistaken. Are you drunk?"

"Counselor! I caution you that another outburst like that and I will find you in contempt!"

"My apologies Your Honour."

A wave of puzzlement wafted over the entire courtroom and a collective suspiration of in-drawn breath hissed through the room. The raised eyebrows and open-mouthed bewilderment of all, including Judge Beeston, was clearly in evidence. As for Kwaku, he, startled and in obvious distress, repeatedly shook his head, speechless at this compounding accusation.

"Order! Order in the court!" The Judge looked at the witness with sternness heretofore unseen in his court. " Miss Carleton, explain yourself!"

"Your Honour, I saw him riding a horse along the Spanish Town road early in the morning of the day the murder is alleged to have been committed." Judge Beeston, realizing his curiosity was getting the better of him, nodded to the prosecutor to continue the questioning.

"How did you manage to be at that location on that day Miss Carleton?"

"On the afternoon of Saturday, February 22, the day before the alleged murder, I was in Spanish Town on business. There I met a wealthy man of some respectability who had to be in Port Royal the next day and since I needed to be there myself, I somewhat reluctantly accepted his offer to travel with him in his two-wheeled trap. As arranged, we stopped at the Ferry Inn for the night. Behind closed doors this man became a monster. He brutally used and abused me physically and emotionally. It took me months to heal from his brutality. He seemed to be angry at the world and himself and took out his frustrations on me, thumping me in the mouth, slapping me across the face, pulling my hair, and throwing me on the ground. Then he took me sexually and not in the usual way, but with the handle of his whip. It was not what we agreed on when first we negotiated the terms of our engagement."

"Objection, Your Honour. This court does not need the sleazy, sordid details of Miss Carleton's activities with one of her many clients."

"Sustained." The judge continued. "The record shows that John Bolt registered at the Ferry Inn the night before the murder, and Miss Carleton just testified that she saw him on the morning of the murder, but we have yet to establish that the man before us today known as Kwaku Johnson is indeed John Bolt. Kwaku Johnson must prove to the court's satisfaction that he was or was not present at the Ferry Inn the night before or on the day of the murder. The accused, please take the stand." Kwaku took his place on the witness stand.

"Your Honour, if I may address the court...."

"Why, Kwaku, you speak like a gentleman, a person of class!" The prosecutor's sarcasm was not lost on Bolt.

"Thank you, gracious sir."

The judge continued. "Are you Kwaku Johnson or are you John Bolt?"

"Sir, I became both." Bolt, handed his manumission papers to the bailiff and turned to the prosecutor. "And no offence intended, counselor, but class is less about being a clothes-horse for the latest fashion, or the prestige of position, or the luxury of money. It is more about personal integrity, respect for all persons, and fair treatment of all human beings. As Kwaku, I have as much class as I have as John Bolt. And now, the only thing that matters between Kwaku Johnson and John Bolt is justice!"

There was silence in the court. The King's English emanating from the persona of a common laborer was startling.

"Were you or were you not at the Ferry Inn on the evening of Saturday, February 22?"

"Your Honour, I was at the Ferry Inn that night."

"And were you on the Spanish Town road the following morning?"

"Yes, Your Honour."

"You realize that that places you circumstantially near the scene of the crime?"

"I do, Your Honour."

"Then, in the matter at hand, it is up to you now, Kwaku Johnson, to prove that you were the John Bolt registered at the Ferry Inn on the night of February 22, 1682, when Miss Carleton and her client were guests there, and that therefore you were the person who the next morning was observed by Miss Carleton on the Spanish Town road.

All eyes shifted back to Bolt.

"This is a long shot, Your Honour, but if Miss Carleton and her client were guests at the Ferry Inn that night, then Miss Carleton may recall hearing me playing a flute on the back steps of my room."

"That was you?" Mary Carleton surprised herself with her outburst.

"Yes, Miss Carleton."

"Your Honour, the hearsay of a person of ill-repute, cannot be sufficient proof of the alibi of the defendant," the prosecutor interjected.

"I would like to confer briefly with my client, Your Honour." Judge Beeston nodded. Richard Long conferred briefly with the defendant who responded with visible apprehension at the communication, but was finally persuaded and defense counsel, with an assuring hand on the shoulder of the defendant, indicated his readiness to continue.

"If I may, Your Honour, in addition to the manumission papers submitted showing this man to be John Bolt, perhaps we can verify this story by a simple test."

"What do you suggest, counselor?"

"If it please the court, let Miss Carleton write down on a tablet the title of one song she recalls hearing that night. Then have Mr. Jo...Mr. Bolt indicate the titles of perhaps three songs. If there is a match, I submit that as sufficient proof of the veracity of these testimonies. The odds of this happening by coincidence, if indeed it does happen, would be astronomical!"

"An unusual proposition, counselor, but under the circumstances....so be it."

Mary Carleton was handed a tablet on which she promptly wrote and handed the tablet to the bailiff who handed it to Judge William Beeston.

"Let the accused stand." Bolt stood nervously. "Name three songs you played that night." Damn. Played at least a dozen songs that night. How the hell am I supposed to....but didn't she lean forward at one point? What song was I playing then?

Bolt hesitated as the court grew impatient, uncomfortable with the silence. The murmur of the crowd grew more pronounced and began to border on open consternation.

"Well? Name at least one song."

"Greensleeves."

Judge William Beeston, both relieved and visibly agitated, turned the tablet around and held it high enough for those in the front rows to see: GREENSLEEVES.

The courtroom erupted first in a collective gasp of surprise, and then like a drizzle of rain progressing to a downpour, the uproar of the crowd became deafening, sustained for several minutes. Finally, Judge Beeston regained his own composure and proceeded to do the same for his court.

"Order! Order in the court! Defense counsel, you may proceed."

"Now, Miss Carleton, you testified that on the night of February 22 you were with a client at the Ferry Inn. This man abused you and battered and brutalized you in most unsavory ways that we need not recount. That man, Miss Carleton, that you speak of: What was his name?"

"His name was Swaby. Justice of the Peace Swaby." There was palpable shock that silenced the courtroom.

"So Miss Carleton, were you the last person to see Justice Swaby alive?" The prosecutor resumed control of the questioning.

"May I remind you, counselor, that Miss Carleton is not on trial here. The defendant is, as we have just now established, John Bolt."

"Point well taken, Your Honour. Miss Carleton, what exactly happened at that now-infamous cotton tree the next morning?"

"Counselor, it was on that morning that I first saw Kwaku....Mr Bolt. Justice Swaby and I were on the Spanish Town Road heading toward Kingston when Mr. Bolt rode past us and later we saw him stopped at the cotton tree where he engaged J.P. Swaby in conversation. I will never forget that voice, so rich and resonant. I could listen to it forever. It was then that I also knew that Mr. Bolt had stayed at the Ferry Inn the night before because the horse I saw standing at the cotton tree had a unique paisley-patterned saddle and matching straps, the same saddle I saw the evening before on a horse that was led to the livery stables and placed alongside the one that drew our trap. I had also seen enough to recognize the same saddle and straps when at first Mr. Bolt rode past us the next day. I knew he had been at the Ferry Inn the night before."

"So, Miss Carleton, what happened between Mr. Bolt and Justice of the Peace Swaby that morning?"

"Mr. Bolt confronted Justice Swaby over his battery of my face. I was hearing Mr. Bolt, a total stranger, as he scolded Swaby for abusing me. It was not long before an altercation ensued between the two men.

Justice Swaby slashed Mr. Bolt in the face with the tip of his whip, and stepped out of the trap with his pistol drawn and another at his waist. Mr. Bolt ducked just as Justice Swaby fired. He missed, but the shot startled Swaby's horse which began moving down the road with me still seated in the trap. I looked back and saw both men scuffling, ending up under the cotton tree. They both fell on the ground and rolled over, when suddenly Justice Swaby, fired again. The second shot must have hit Bolt's horse because it reared up and came down, one hoof landing squarely on Swaby's head, and the other narrowly missing Bolt himself."

"So, you are testifying that Justice Swaby's death was accidental?"

"Yes, Your Honour. It was an accident. I saw it all. Months later, when a vendor with a scruffy beard, a more sunburned face, and shabby clothes, called at my establishment, I at first paid no special attention, but despite his use of the local patois, that voice was unmistakable. A closer look was enough to confirm my suspicions. I knew the man calling himself Kwaku was in fact John Bolt, but I said nothing."

"How could you recognize him and he not recognize you?"

"Sir, when Mr. Bolt saw me along the Spanish Town Road I had a fat lip and one of my eyes was damned near closed from swelling after that brute had his way with me. Later, after I had recovered, and the swelling was gone, I cut my hair short and dyed it to this auburn shade to escape suspicion for the murder of Justice of the Peace Swaby. I am not surprised that Kwaku...Mr.Bolt didn't recognize me."

"Miss Carleton, why did you not give this information to the authorities? You knew like everyone else that the coroner's inquest yielded very little except that blunt force was the probable cause of death, no gunshot wounds being evident on the body. Why did you not report this information?"

""With all due respect, your Honour, I didn't want to draw attention to myself for this would likely make me a suspect, being one of the last to see Justice Swaby alive. And, furthermore, as Your Honour can appreciate, in my line of business secrecy is paramount. As I am sure Your Honour would agree." At this Judge William Beeston turned visibly red. The veiled threat evident in the oral inflections of Mary Carleton was sufficient to give him pause.

Anxious to abandon this line of exchange, Judge Beeston decided on another direction of questioning. "The defendant will take the stand." Bolt calmly stood, walking with deliberate steps as befits a person of better breeding, his gait a contradiction of the plainness of his attire.

"Mr. Bolt, as the last person to see Justice Swaby alive, it seemed mighty suspicious that you would choose to disappear and assume another identity. Were you not aware of this?"

"Your Honour, as a freedman but a Negro nevertheless, I did not feel then and I still have my doubts now, that my story would be believed since it involved the death of a European. I had been long enough in Spanish Town, the seat of power on this island, to know this." Robert long rose to address the judge.

"Your Honour, whereas the death of Justice of the Peace Archibald Swaby has been demonstrated by eyewitness testimony to have been accidental, I respectfully move dismissal of all charges against my client."

Judge Beeston momentarily hesitated as the crowd waited.

The gavel came down with resounding finality. "Agreed. Mr. Bolt, you are a free man. This court is adjourned!"

Bolt embraced Robert Long and then Mary Carleton as the prosecutor, thoroughly disgusted at the outcome of events, retreated, the crowd parting in silence to let him pass, and erupting in cheers as Bolt, Long, and Miss Carleton left together. Reverend Heath and Poincie were awaiting him outside the building and the three hugged enthusiastically. Bolt thanked Reverend Heath effusively for his help in securing the services of Robert Long, and explained that he and Long needed to confer further before Bolt could return to Port Royal.

Poincie, tears of relief still streaming down her cheeks, chided him, pummeling him in the chest with both fists:

"You rascal you! You fool all o'we. I never knew. You got me so worried." Then she buried her head in his chest, hugging him, as if her very life depended on it, desperately trying to sort out a jumble of overlapping emotions.

"I tried to tell you about all this at Reverend Heath's house, remember?" "Yes, but still..." Poincie hugged him tighter.

When finally they bade him goodbye, Poincie said,

"See you soon Kwaku...er... Mr. Bolt."

"No problem Putoos! You can call me anyting you want!"

Reverend Heath waved, smiling, and then, blessing him with the sign of the cross, said in his best attempt at patois, "Walk good, Mr. Bolt!" It was the most heart-felt blessing he had ever given.

"Walk good, Reverend Heath."

As Reverend Heath and Poincie made their way back to Port Royal, Poincie became calm and introspective. Reverend Heath could sense her pensive mood and did not intrude on her reverie as their carriage lumbered along the road, each person lost in thought. John Bolt. Or Kwaku. Poincie smiled as she thought of Kwaku, that lovable rascal who told her naughty Anancy stories and taught her to love the earth and respect Mother Nature. He had taught her to respect people from every walk of life, not judging worth from appearance but from values and character. Kwaku had rugged hands and his hugs were tight and heart-warming. Poincie sensed the quiet strength forming the basis for his tenderness. She giggled when he teased her good- naturedly, savoring the attention that he lavished on her on his visits, always wishing he would linger longer.

Now that Kwaku was revealed as John Bolt, Poincie saw more clearly some of the qualities that were merely hinted at in Kwaku. He was so knowledgeable and had firm convictions on justice, so well spoken and eloquent, treating a lady with all the social graces any woman would want. His bravery in defending Mary Carleton was admirable even given his lack of awareness of who she was, although he may have seen her as another victim of an oppressive social hierarchy. Poincie smiled and reaffirmed to herself what she had known all along: "Regardless, me love dis man."

Robert Long and Mary Carleton, both of whom remained in Spanish Town, secured for Bolt the proper clothing and footwear appropriate to a gentleman before the three repaired to the anonymity of a darkened pub on a side street near the square. They spent some time reflecting on the day's developments. Bolt had intended to pay for his new outfit, now that he had access to his savings in a local bank, but Long and Carleton insisted on treating him to a short shopping expedition.

Robert Long wanted to know, "Miss Carleton, how did you become a witness for the prosecution?"

"Perhaps, even more important is why," suggested Bolt.

"Look Bolt, I knew from early on that you were not Kwaku. I know enough of men to know when there is something slightly out of kilter. I sensed a certain mannerism or demeanor that said, 'This is no common man, no common laborer.' Later, when I realized who you were, I saw in you my defender, my savior, from that brute Swaby. I thought long and hard how your innocence could never be established on your word alone. You would for the rest of your life be a fugitive at best, and more than likely end up dancing in the breeze at Port Royal. I had to do something, so when I heard that Kwaku was on trial for murder, I volunteered as a witness to save you from that fate, telling the prosecutor that I had information about your true identity. That is why he asked if you were a freedman and for proof of your status. I know this man (don't ask me how); he was all about himself. He was hoping to make a name for himself by exposing a bigger criminal than a mere laborer. I let on that I could and would incriminate you, telling him everything except the fact that I saw the horse stomp down on Swaby's head. In his mind, putting you there at the scene as the last person to see Swaby alive was generally sufficient to establish your guilt. But I vowed in my mind to exonerate you."

"That was quite a gamble, wasn't it?"

"Of course. But what was I to lose? In a few days I depart for England. My establishment will be taken over by an associate. My passage is already booked. If my ruse failed, and if you were convicted, then you would hate me, but I would be gone, never to return. It was worth the risk."

"Miss Carleton...."

"Call me Mary."

"Mary, why did the prosecutor bring charges against me as Kwaku?"

"A man from Stokes Hall Estate. A man named Bradford."

"I see."

Robert Long looked at them both and shook his head. "Mary Carleton, you are quite something else." Bolt looked at Mary Carleton. In another time and place, under different circumstances, one might have mistaken her for a noblewoman. Bolt arose and she did the same. They embraced, tightly and prolonged, unashamedly. She held him still close to her, kissed him tenderly on both cheeks, and looked into his eyes. "Goodbye, Mr. Bolt."

CHAPTER TWENTY-FIVE

Walk Good, Kwaku.

John Bolt smiled to himself as he rounded the corner of a side street in Spanish Town. The sign was still there: Horses for Hire. It was a convenient service to hire a horse, leave it at the Ferry Inn, or at stables in Kingston or Port Royal where others could hire the same for a ride in the opposite direction. He asked for a horse fitted with an ornate saddle, decorated with patterns of paisley. The livery attendant obliged knowingly, since news of the trial and his exoneration had become chitchat in households and on the streets. He started out on his journey just as the dusty curtain of evening began to descend on the landscape. It was easy to be lost in a reverie, recalling recent events as, once again, he rode briskly along the Spanish Town Road. It was on this road some years before that his life had taken a strange and unexpected turn. Life could be so uncertain. He hoped to reach the Ferry Inn before deepening darkness made the ride dangerous.

Horse and rider developed a healthy gallop silhouetted against the orange hues of sunset as they charged down the graveled road. Bolt was anxious to pass a section of heavily wooded roadway where highwaymen were known to accost travellers. They rounded a corner of the road, both horse and rider leaning into the apex as they endeavored to maintain the same momentum achieved on the straightway. But then, involuntarily, the horse abruptly skidded to a halt, reared up on its hind legs, neighing in surprise.

Bolt pulled on the reins to avoid falling backward off his mount, and as they settled back on all fours he saw the cause of the alarm. In the middle of the road stood a tall shrub, leaves rustling, but the specter itself immobile. A tree in the middle of the road. This was unusual. The Maroons had talked about warriors using leafy camouflage but he had never seen this for himself. If this was a Maroon in camouflage then there would be many others and this also meant imminent attack. Maroons always travelled in groups. Furthermore, as Kwaku he would not be afraid, but as John Bolt he would be a prime target. He looked quickly, anxiously, in both directions. It was a lonely road, and he was on that heavily wooded stretch, the road now shrouded in shadow.

"Hallo!" No answer. "HALLO!" No response. "WHA GWAAN?"

There was an uneasy silence. Then from the leaves came laughter, the raucous laughter of a woman. She caught her breath and laughed again. The upper section of leaves folded down to reveal a young black woman. Her shoulders were bare, and her head was covered in a dark green wrap which framed her face and was tied in the back by a giant butterfly knot, both ends sticking out and visible on either side of her tall neck. She had prominent cheekbones, a resolute mouth, and piercing eyes that seemed to look not so much at as through a person.

"You can come dung from de horse, Kwaku." It was as much a command as a request. Bolt complied, standing by the horse, the reins still in his hands.

"We glad fe you, Kwaku."

"You know me?"

"You no know me, but we know you. A so we like it."

Kwaku had heard his contacts make mention of a woman Maroon, a Queen Nanny. Could this be her?

"You was at de trial?"

"Yah man. We everywhere. We know wha happen a de court. We know everyting dat happen. And we stan' fe justice. We know seh you get off today. Is dat mek we happy fe you."

Bolt Nodded. "So what if me neva did get off?"

"We 'ave we ways. You no worry 'bout dat." With that she gestured unobtrusively and the road darkened for some distance as from both sides dozens of warriors emerged fully bushed and lined up in two phalanxes behind the woman.

Bolt nodded and an ever-broadening smile spread across his face. "Me see wha' you mean."

She reached into the leaves and produced a pouch from which she withdrew a thin leather cord from which dangled the incisor tooth of a wild boar.

"Chief Cudjoe sen you dis." She came closer, reached over, and placed the necklace around his neck.

"Thank you. Tell him me will wear it wid pride. And, who are you?"

"De English call me Nanny of the Maroons. You can jus' call me Nanny. Walk good, Kwaku."

With that she turned, stepped aside to let him pass, and the two phalanxes of warriors separated. Bolt held the reins, leading the horse as he walked through the middle. Behind him he heard the crunch of the horse's hooves accompanied by a barely perceptible rustle of leaves, and as he approached, each warrior raised a machete, jonga, or assegai high in the air as he nodded acknowledgement. Once through, he remounted the horse and whipped its head around with a swift jerk of the reins, intending to wave goodbye to the group. The road was empty.

Bolt fingered the boar's tooth momentarily, tucked it safely inside his shirt, and charged off into the evening. He arrived at the Ferry Inn after dark and lay on his bed, thoughts still galloping through his head.

Now, where did he go from here? The conversation he had had with Attorney Robert Long today after the trial was intriguing, to say the least. After Mary Carleton had taken her leave and Bolt and Long were reflecting on the day's events over another pint of ale, Long had said,

"That's quite a feat you pulled off, John. You had me and everyone else completely in the dark."

"Not so much by choice as of necessity, Mr. Long."

"Call me Robert. May I call you John?"

"Of course. And Robert, I owe you my life. I will never be able to repay you."

"You know, of course, that Reverend Heath insisted we represent you."

"I owe him so much too."

"You know, John, I was thinking about how you conducted yourself on the stand as a defendant. Both as Kwaku and as John Bolt you were quite articulate and forceful. You would make a good advocate. And did you see the response of the crowd when you spoke?

"I...I don't know....what are you suggesting?"

"I am thinking that with your skill with figures and accounting and speaking, if you were a clerk in my firm, and eventually articled, you could one day be an attorney. It would be a long shot but think about it."

"That would give me a chance to work off the expense of my defense, these fine clothes and help me to help some other unfortunates. I most certainly will think about it. Thank you."

And think about it he would, and maybe Poincie too could get a position in Montego Bay....

Bolt decided to spend a few days at the Ferry Inn before moving on past Kingston to Port Royal. With his newfound notoriety he was recognized almost everywhere he went and needed a brief respite from people and the emotionally charged days of the trial and its aftermath. This time when he checked into the Inn, the innkeeper recognized him immediately and gave him the best room on the second floor, ensuring that the noise of the tavern and the smell of rum would not be intrusive. He would catch the Royal Mail stagecoach and return to Port Royal when he felt sufficiently rested.

Chapter Twenty-Six

Marshalsea Prison

It was another Friday morning, June the sixth, 1692, and Reverend Heath travelled to the Marshalsea Prison where he would minister to one Lewis Galdy, his former barber recently charged with piracy, who would perhaps shortly face his fate dangling from the end of the rope at Gallows Point. Often in Port Royal, justice, or what masqueraded as justice, was meted out in speedy fashion. A man could be tried and summarily hanged in the same day. An accused pirate like Galdy would be quickly dispatched.

Visiting prison inmates accused of piracy was the least pleasurable of Heath's duties. Even a funeral was better than this since the latter had the feeling of closure, of resolution, a culmination of a life, while the prospect of imminent death was a painful sense of foreboding and dread without finality but the bitter realization of impending doom.

Heath would offer any words of comfort he could afford, speak in terms that Galdy could understand, with no hint of the inner agnosticism which Heath had long since come to acknowledge in himself. His duty was to bring comfort to the bereaved and the distressed, to add affirmation to the important rites of passage. He steeled himself as he approached the dreadful place.

The Marshalsea Prison was a depressing place to say the least. He had been there before when Kwaku had been confined within those walls before his trial. It was a red brick structure with walls at least two feet thick and doors framed in dark, stout bullet wood. Dark, narrow halls with low ceilings like catacombs extended into dark, dank obscurity. Heath approached Galdy's cell with a warden escort who locked them in and left to return after the designated time allowed for visitors.

The cell was dank and smelled of mildew and the stench of a marsh, rather like the smooth grey- walled interior of a derelict water tank and just as morass-laden. A concrete slab was Galdy's bed and a tin plate with partly eaten mush lay on the floor. The only light was from a narrow, deeply recessed window some twelve inches square with vertical iron bars inches apart. Heath thought of the twists and turns of what constituted Galdy's life, a life whose days were numbered. This was not what Galdy had envisioned when he left his native France hoping for a new beginning in the New World.

Galdy must have pulled himself up by those bars and peered out at the thin horizontal sliver of ocean afforded by his effort and to his left a glimpse of Gallows Point. Eventually his arms could no longer endure the strain of supporting his body and he let go and surrendered to gravity, crumpling to the ground. He was in this fetal posture when he was greeted by the warden and Reverend Heath.

"Get up! You scoundrel! You have a visitor."

"Thank you Warden. Mr. Galdy, it's Reverend Heath."

"Hi Reverend. Right decent of you to come."

"Sorry about your situation Lewis. I understand that tomorrow you may be tried for piracy."

"Aye, Reverend. Never thought my life would come to this *t'sais*? I could be swinging from Gallows Point tomorrow."

"Ah Lewis. Life is not always fair. But when you first came to worship at St. Paul's you were not into piracy were you?"

"No Reverend. At first I tried honest labor. Tried to make a go of it. In Port Royal if you didn't operate a tavern, run a whorehouse, or be in the militia, then ye only chance to make a life was to go to sea either as a sailor or a pirate. As a white man I could easily work on a sugar plantation as an overseer, but slavery goes against the grain for me, since freedom was why I left France. I could not countenance the thought of profiting from the bondage of other human beings, black or white *t'sais*? As you know, I even tried barbering for a while."

"So you turned to piracy?"

"*Entre nous* Reverend, on a pirate ship we have a say. We can decide who our leader is. We choose the captain most of the time. We have rules of fair play and the sharing of the booty. We put our mark on a covenant before we set sail. We have our own government on that boat."

"It's a floating democracy."

"*Exactment*, Reverend. Granted, ours was not a pleasant business. We showed no mercy when we boarded a Spanish ship. We were instruments of God's justice. Slitting a throat or running a man through was not a cause for any regret. It was kill or be killed. *T'sais*, I was used to shaving men's throats. It was but a short step to slitting them. Still, there were times when I reflected on how I came to be in this dastardly mess called piracy. It was not conducive to my nature. There were times I felt more like an animal than a man. And like an animal I could hang tomorrow...."

`Galdy and Heath commiserated until the warden intervened and they said their fervent prayers and their goodbyes, hoping that the great unknown would reward them with another opportunity to greet each other in infinity or whatever lay beyond. It was a parting not without tears.

Heath reflected on the unfairness of it all. When the Crown found it advantageous, piracy was encouraged and rewarded. Then it was punishable by hanging when deemed inopportune. Galdy was a mere pawn in a game played by capricious royals. A hastily called court proceeding in Spanish Town would be convened and precipitously concluded; all that would be left for Galdy's immediate execution would be the signature of the new governor who was known to casually sign such orders between mere syllables of conversation with his cronies. The order could come at any moment and Galdy would be taken forthwith from Marshalsea to Gallows Point to swing in the breeze like so many other unfortunates before him.

Chapter Twenty-Seven

Revelry and Rivalry

The Colonial Council decided to relocate the governor of Jamaica from Port Royal to Spanish Town, the capital, where a more elaborate residence was provided for him. The former Governor's Mansion in Port Royal was, however, an imposing three-story stone structure set back from a semi-circular driveway on High Street. It was a very desirable venue for formal occasions such as a ball or banquet for the well-to-do such as the recently arrived Lord Stokes of Stokes Hall.

On the grassy area enclosed by the driveway was a tri-level fountain of drab grey stone with tall earthenware jars arranged around it, each jar with flowers of various hues spilling over the edges. The columned ironwork gates having been opened wide, a steady stream of horse-drawn carriages could be seen entering the driveway and pulling up to the entrance where gloved and uniformed attendants opened doors for the easy egress of the well-to-do and directed the drivers as to where to park and wait, possibly till the morning, when some would choose to leave.

Reverend Heath, riding with John White in his carriage, arrived and ascended the impressive steps that led to the second floor and into the main ballroom. The lower level of the mansion was occupied with offices and functions of less glamorous import.

The ballroom was an opulent, cavernous space with tall windows draped floor-to-ceiling in elegant silks and satins of burgundy and bottle green. The ceiling was divided into neat squares, each with its own intricate pattern of shapes and colors and each deeply recessed, requiring substantial light to appreciate fully its individual uniqueness. This light was supplied by three massive chandeliers, equally spaced along the center of the ceiling and each like an upside-down waterfall of dazzling crystals casting an enchanting glow on the ceiling above and on the finery of the revelers below.

Likewise, underfoot were rugs, carpets and runners of intricate design and subdued colors. Along the walls were portraits of somber well-dressed dignitaries, women of ample proportions, and young women with pale, almost transparent skin that seemed never to have seen the light of day.

Heath scanned the room and recognized many distinguished men and women, peers of Lord Stokes, all come to pay their respects. Among them there were planters and their wives from the nearby properties such as Hampton Court Estate, Golden Grove, Duckenfield Hall, Holland Estates, Amity Hall, Winchester and Wheelerfield. There were also some government officials and civil servants as well as some overseers, George Bradford included. Jack Hart remained behind at Stokes Hall..

On the estates there was an unspoken understanding that given the small number of Europeans and the much larger negro population, upper class whites would accommodate those of lower station in life for mutual support, and even protection, despite the knowledge that if circumstances were different the two classes would not be so closely associated. It was a tribal necessity to occasionally treat social inferiors as equals. It was an awkward accommodation in which neither group took much pleasure.

At first Heath noticed that each man of significant influence was surrounded by a cluster of both men and women of lesser station, each vying for the attention of the distinguished personage, the latter indicating by the size of his circle of acquaintances the level of influence and prestige he enjoyed. Later, as the evening wore on, there would be a coming together of the true elite, at which time persons of lesser station would not have access and would keep their respectable distance. It was a crowd dynamic that Heath consciously recognized and was a source of private bemusement as he studied the enduring dynamics of the English planter culture in this new island context.

Soon the guests were summoned from the antechamber into the formal dining room where tables were set in a U-shaped configuration, place settings meticulously arranged with identical napkins, utensils, plates, fingerbowls, and stemware. Lord Stokes himself sat in the apex of the U with John White and other members of the Colonial Council beside him, as well as other distinguished guests, all radiating from the left and right of Lord Stokes. Lord Luke Stokes, his father now deceased, had been the governor of Nevis before his death, and now the younger Stokes seemed to have been accorded the same deference as his forbear.

The organizers of this reception spared no expense, securing the finest food that Port Royal could offer. Guests had their choice of roast beef, stewed mudfish, pickled crab, fried liver, roast pork, stewed hogshead, plantain pudding, watermelon, oranges, varieties of rum from various estates, French brandy, pawpaw, fresh potatoes, shrimps, roast goose, stewed fish, and plum pudding. The party dined in splendor, served by uniformed mulatto and Negro servants all properly trained to answer to every beck and call. John White clumsily dropped a fork beside his chair and on reaching down to retrieve it, discovered the hand of a servant already there and a replacement already beside his plate as he looked up again.

There was lively banter and exchanges of pleasantries with Lord Stokes himself, the latter taking the opportunity to bring the latest news of developments in England and describing political and social trends in the homeland. It was a tour de force of nostalgia and he relished the interaction. It was a far cry from the dull existence of rural England. Being a recognized member of the Jamaican plantocracy was splendid indeed. He began to be grateful for the decision to return to Stokes Hall, if only for a visit.

Meanwhile, an ensemble of string musicians tuned their instruments and prepared to entertain the assemblage. They began to play as tea was served. Johann Sebastian Bach, Claudio Monteverdi, Michael Wise, John Hilton and others were represented in musical presence, their cadences pressed into elegant service that was a balm for the ears and eyes, for soon the waltzes brought people to their feet. In the main ballroom they began to dance, led by the illustrious Lord Stokes. The women, their hair of suitably coiffed, wore long flowing gowns of satin, lacy cotton, and velvet trim. They floated around the room guided deftly by their escorts like swans on a ripple-free pond. The variety of textures and colors all moving gracefully in kaleidoscopic splendor was a pleasure to onlookers like Heath who was content to be entertained, watching from the sidelines.

Presently, the music became faster-paced and more aerobic as some of the recent French jigs were played. Some whose tastes were more conducive to indulging in this art form joined in and all were having a jolly good time. Their vigorous exertions were almost taxing to watch as flailing arms and intricate fast-paced footwork dazzled the more sedate onlookers. Dresses swirled, coiled around the legs and ankles, unfurling in carefree abandon, revealing fringes of lacy petticoats, only to repeat like the incessant ebb and flow of the tide.

Some younger men, anxious to show their familiarity with the latest dances coming from Europe, seemed competing with each other, impressing the ladies. Young Lord Stokes himself, only newly arrived from England, seemed quite adept at showing his familiarity with various dances, taking turns in demonstrating his finesse with several ladies in turn, each anxious to have their chance to have his attention. The atmosphere began to have a somewhat riotous overtone as abundant wine and rum began to dance in their heads.

Reverend Heath scanned the opulent ballroom, looked around at the revelers and unintentionally murmured to himself.

"When the chicken is merry, the hawk is near."

"Pardon me? What is this about a hawk?" John White, who was standing nearby with champagne glass in hand had overheard the brief soliloquy.

"Oh, never mind. An old folk proverb. It is time I take my leave. I have early morning prayers tomorrow at St Paul's."

"My driver will take you home."

"Thanks, but that won't be necessary. I need to walk to gather my thoughts."

"I'll be at the Crown and Anchor tomorrow morning. Please join me after prayers, Reverend." Heath nodded in agreement and walked away.

John White himself did not long remain at the ball. It was generally understood that after certain personages had departed the company, the celebration would take on a more hedonistic tone, a more Bacchanalian flavor in which the rules of polite decorum were progressively suspended as the night wore on.

Had he stayed behind he would have noticed when the music transitioned into a more seductive, languorous rhythm and tone as the dancers gradually abandoned the more detached and proper postures and became more engaging, more expressive, more proximate in the interactions of their bodies. It would not be long before the entire assemblage would disengage, and approach three tables on which were stacked masks of every variety and design. Each person would don the mask of his or her choice, and the lights of the ballroom were lowered by extinguishing the chandeliers, leaving those lights on the sidewalls only.

Then the revelers mingled in reckless abandon, dancing, drinking, flirting, playing, and then copulating in every form, fashion, fetish, and fantasy. Hallways, side rooms, privies, bedrooms, lounges, scullery, balcony, every venue was fair game, and every masked persona encountered became an intriguing mystery to be probed, explored, and plumbed.

The revelry continued far into the night, and as the morning approached there were still some, Lord Stokes included, who lingered in debauched disarray, some with masks still on, some without, splayed on and under tables and couches, beds, and floors, half asleep, drunk, passed out, in a variety of poses and postures and in various stages of dress and undress. They would sleep off the after-effects of their night and then depart for home before noon. Or, so they thought.

CHAPTER TWENTY-EIGHT

The Earthquake

Gatha looked out through the kitchen window on the morning of Saturday, June 7,1692. She wiped the sweat from her forehead with the back of her hand, repositioned the scarf on her head and grabbed her hip for a moment. This was a different ache than she was accustomed to coping with. More intense. Different. Arthritis? Maybe. She hurriedly finished washing the pots and pans, put them away and started on the breakfast dishes, cups, and trays. Yesterday she had noticed that the moon had been veiled by a dark layer of cloud unlike anything she had seen in recent memory. It was a blood moon. She recalled having heard the older folks and even Kwaku refer to a "bad moon." Could this be what they meant?

That night her apprehensions gave rise to a nightmare with an evil eye leering at the silhouetted forms of a dire and desolate landscape. She prematurely awoke when the pain demanded her attention but managed to prepare breakfast for Reverend Heath and sent him and Poincie off to early Saturday prayer service at St. Paul's. Services were held early to allow parishioners to retreat to the shade of their houses before the oppressive heat bore full force on the landscape. As she gathered the breakfast things she felt herself sway and she almost lost her footing. Only by pressing her elbow against the doorjamb did she manage to right herself and continue into the walkway leading to the kitchen.

But what is dis! I getting so old, I ca'an even walk steady. De grung feel like it movin'.

Another early morning prayer service over, the Reverend Heath stood at the door of St Paul's church and shook the hands of his parishioners as they departed through the front door. He bade Poincie goodbye as she returned to the rectory and Gatha. His homily that morning was on Jonah and the baptism and born-again experience that Jonah's experience exemplified. The last parishioner's hand shaken and pleasantries exchanged, Reverend Heath surrendered his clerical collar and proceeded to walk to the Crown and Anchor to meet with his friend John White, President of the Colonial Council. The two men chatted over a bottle of Wormwood wine while White smoked his pipe of tobacco. Heath was reluctant to leave his friend until the pipe was sufficiently exhausted.

Suddenly, the entire tavern seemed to creak as the walls and floorboards shuddered and squirmed. Heath looked quizzically at White.

"Lord, Sir, what is this?"

"A mere tremor, my friend. Don't be afraid. 'Twill soon be over."

A sudden stillness descended like a lull in the conversation when a person of nobility enters a room, but this was to be a terrible visitation. Reverend Heath glanced at the grandfather clock in the corner of the Crown and Anchor and noted the time. It was 11:43 a.m. Heath had but a fleeting moment when he looked out the latticed window on a mirror-glass sea where it met a copper-hued horizon. Other patrons at the Crown and Anchor, having felt the sudden heaving of the floor of the tavern were instantly on high alert, flagons raised only halfway to their mouths.

A second heaving, longer this time, came like a giant awakening from unpleasant nightmarish sleep. The third convulsion seemed continuous as if the world was retching to hurl the vomit of her moral indigestion, and hell itself was in uproar!Reverend Heath gasped in terror as he dashed out of the Crown and Anchor through a doorway now severely distorted as ceiling beams yielded to the pressure of terrible forces. He looked in the direction of St. Paul's and saw the tower take leave of the roof and the church implode into a pile of rubble, then dissolve into the liquefaction. The land flexed like mounds and dunes, imitating the waves. As Heath looked down Queen Street, he saw buildings erratically bobbing up and down like corks in a water basin before they disintegrated.

The buildings swayed like drunkards on the heaving earth and then sank like rocks below its surface. Others leaned and yielded to the shocks as they keeled over with crushing finality mingling sand and soil, sea and blood, flesh and wood, mortar and bone all in one cataclysmic convulsion.

Heath's first thought after his initial shock was for the fate of Gatha, Poincie, and his dwelling.

But nature was not yet satiated. Heath watched as the sea receded as if to step back and concentrate its rage. The receding waves clawed at the land, scraping the remnants of St. Paul's out to sea. Eventually yielding to the superior force of nature, the grave of Sir Henry Morgan surrendered its wooden coffin and once again Henry Morgan, triumphant in death, rode the waves. Then a wall of water several stories high returned with a vengeance and inundated the landscape, sweeping everything in its wake before eventually receding, leaving nothing but despair and destruction behind it. The fury was unabated for all of three seemingly interminable minutes.

Later, as Heath viewed the devastation he noticed Backra Bradford's face, blue and still above the ground, being chewed on by wild dogs. Heath turned aside, retched and vomited over the odious specter. Two thirds of what had been Port Royal was nowhere to be seen. Of what was left of the land it was a scene of utter devastation. Where once stood an imposing residence there was now a ship, broken and derelict swept landward and dumped by the tsunami. Others having similarly dragged their anchors, were sitting in various states of disarray across streets and yards. One such vessel, the HMS Swan was swept inland and dumped by the tsunami, but managed to remain upright. About two hundred desperate souls clambered aboard her and were saved when the next wave bore the ship back out to sea. Children's bodies like rag dolls littered the sand and corpses half-buried lay strewn in various postures of disarray. Noah would have wept.

But it wasn't yet over. A new wave, this of the human kind, swept over the scene. Thieves and brigands, barely overcoming their own initial shock, descended like vultures and began robbing the dead bodies strewn over the landscape. The task of forcing a ring off a finger, being too arduous, some merely chopped off the finger to free the ring. Others dove into the still tumultuous water to retrieve treasures submerged in the homes of the wealthy. Human scavengers scoured the land in search of filthy lucre. Even the survivors scavenging their own wrecked homes, those fortunate enough to be spared sinking into the massive quicksand, yielded to the demands of looters who relieved them of their few salvaged artifacts or family heirlooms.

From behind the bars of Marshalsea Men's Prison Lewis Galdy had looked out on High Street. Not a stone's throw away was the courthouse where he would no doubt be convicted of the crime of piracy, and behind that was Gallows Point where he would hang for his crime. Across the street was Bridewell Prison for the confinement of female unfortunates. As Galdy dejectedly contemplated his fate, his cell shuddered and the floor convulsed, throwing him against the wall. He staggered like a drunk trying to find his sea legs on the heaving deck of a ship battered by an angry ocean. A glance through the barred window showed sea and land both flow and wave like one continuum commingling. Fissures gaped wide and closed. Grown men screamed like children, their cries muffled as the earth opened and swallowed them whole.

The prison wall caved inward barely missing Galdy's head as he ducked and crawled through an opening that a moment before had been a locked doorway. He staggered out of his prison into the confinement of nature. Here where time and nature, chance and circumstance, held sway, he was at their mercy. A fissure opened before Galdy. He looked at the innards of the earth and staggered back arresting his advance just as another opened under him and he was swallowed into the bowels of the earth and all was blackness. He was dust and to dust he had returned. The earth contracted like a lung around him and in deadly embrace encompassed him, then like a lung opened and expelled him back into the open air as the land washed out to sea.

Galdy quickly regained consciousness and thrashed about in the watery mass grave until two lads in a canoe hauled him screaming hysterically into their boat and calmed him down. They helped him ashore as he wandered in a daze, trying to make sense of the utter devastation he had just been a part of. Others were not so lucky. He observed one pirate who was half-swallowed by a fissure and in a strait-jacket of earth just as the tsunami came rushing on land and mercifully drowned him.

There was a peculiar groan, a rumble, a deep-throated roar that emanated seemingly from the bowels of the earth. It startled the slaves, the free Negroes, the pirates, the whores and even the animals, as the sea birds rose into the air in panicked disarray. Without warning, the entire island of Jamaica shrugged, nay shivered, an ever-swelling trembling, then a quivering and convulsing as the land was racked with multiple earth spasms and all was embroiled in turmoil and confusion. Up in the mountain country the Maroons swayed like drunken brawlers while children ran in panic, clinging to the legs and frocks of their mothers. The slaves on the sugar estates paused to stare vainly at each other in puzzlement, everyone--- drivers, field hands, house servants, and madeira-sipping backras equally bewildered and helpless as Mother Nature asserted her overarching will. The quake intensified as it moved with incredible speed like a battalion of invisible giants across the land, kneading the ground, shuffling rocks and boulders alike, and waving the trees like the banners of a dreadfully triumphant army.

John Bolt had taken the early morning stagecoach to Port Royal. As the coach rumbled along, the first outlines of the city became visible, then it suddenly felt as if the large carriage wheels had turned to flexible rubber as the coach rode up and bottomed out on a roadway that seemed transformed into a rolling sea. The horses themselves were in a panic whinnying and seeming to be at cross-purposes to each other with the driver struggling to control one and then the other and finally bringing both to a halt while shouting to the passengers to disembark immediately. Bolt disembarked and looked ahead while the ground repeatedly shrugged, like an old man endeavoring to dislodge an irritant on his back. There, not five yards ahead, was a fissure running diagonally across the road. The driver and other passengers were in a state of confusion, muttering, questioning, praying, and remonstrating when Bolt left them on foot. He had to find his way to the rectory. Mary Carleton would have left for England already.

Bolt cast his eyes from the yellow sky and ominous dark clouds to scan the land below, only to see buildings like so many pebbles scattered by a careless hand and sinking out of sight in a marshy morass. All that section below High Street simply disappeared while those above danced the evil dance of destruction. Then, as he looked he seemed to see a mountain range coming toward the devastated city, a moving range of what he came to realize was not a land mass but a wall of water several stories high judging from the remembered heights of buildings that were no longer there. It swept inland sweeping everything in the harbor landward, depositing ships where large buildings once stood. He had to find out if Poincie, and Gatha and the reverend were safe. Possibly their location near the fort on the higher elevations of Port Royal might mean that they survived if anyone could survive this massive natural upheaval. He must find his way there. He must find his way to the rectory.

As Bolt got closer he realized more clearly the utter devastation that had overtaken Port Royal. Gone. Two thirds of the city, gone, sunk below the waves. And of what still remained, streets, houses, offices, boats, coffins, bodies, glass, wood, iron, zinc sheeting, utensils, glassware, pieces of eight, currency of all nationalities, tableware, exotic textiles, trunks, jewelry, shoes, clothing, every artifact of human civilization seemed to have been gathered into one giant mixing bowl and crushed, mangled, pulverized and soaked into a homogenized witches brew of death and destruction splashed over an apocalyptic landscape. He stepped over the debris and realizing he should be near the place where the Governor's mansion once stood, he peered around a mound of refuse and to his surprise, realized it still stood. At least a part of it was recognizable.

Bolt was afforded a closer look as he hastened slowly through the building on his way toward the rectory. Sure enough, although the walls were window-less, the outer stone walls still stood. The building had collapsed from within, the roof and floors giving way and leaving the outer shell of the building to keep up appearances. Bolt gingerly tiptoed through the rubble, the beams, the broken glass, and spotted a smashed violin.

Around him were vultures of the human kind, looters already relieving the dead bodies of the nobility of all jewelry, currency, and other valuables and taking their clothes and finery. A heavy chandelier, now in shambles, was being lifted by two ne'er-do-wells. Underneath, as the loose crystals cascaded down on a dead body, Bolt saw the empty stare of the partially clothed man. One of the brigands who helped lift the chandelier grabbed the lifeless hand and, twisting and pulling, tried in vain to remove the ring from the index finger.

It was an elaborate piece, with sapphires forming the backdrop for the large stylized S rendered in gold, as was the rest of the ring that framed it. Presently the robber reached into his pocket, drew out a crude blade and proceeded to saw back and forth, hacking through the finger, eventually freeing the ring. John Bolt had seen that stylized S before. He had furtively glimpsed it on a wall-mounted plaque in the living room of Stokes Hall as he glanced through a side window on his way to the kitchen at the back. Young Lord Stokes' body lay there partially clothed with the nude bodies of two women like discarded ragdolls on each side. Bolt recognized them as Mary Carleton's girls whom he had seen on one of his visits. He had seen enough. He must leave the facade and find his way to the rectory. Reverend Heath would not be happy to hear of the tragic end of his young friend.

At the rectory Poincie had been dusting the bookshelves of the study, reminiscing on the talks she had had with Heath, the books, mainly on theology, she had read. When she felt the first shudderings of the quake, her immediate reflex was to grasp the shelf to steady herself, but the latter began to spill its books, hitting Poincie in the face and scattering its contents on the floor. Soon Poincie found herself on the floor being covered by falling books and finally she looked up to see the bookshelf itself tottering and eventually falling toward her. It was all she could do to cover her head with folded arms and absorb the impact. She felt a sharp pain at the back of her neck and realized that she must have lost consciousness momentarily. She managed to extricate herself from the weight of the shelf and the books that partially buried her.

When she ascertained that a bruise and a minor concussion were her most serious injuries, she hurried out to see how Gatha had fared. "Aunt Gatha?" she yelled. "You all right?" When she received no answer, she dashed toward the kitchen, but not without difficulty because the back door from the rectory would not open. She tried in vain to shoulder it open but it was firmly jammed. Poincie climbed through a side window, the panes having shattered as the frame became distorted, and ignored the scrapes and bruises sustained from shards of splintered glass.

First, she caught sight of Gatha's cottage, and realized it had collapsed, looking like a crumped-up wad of paper that a writer had squashed and thrown away. Then she saw the kitchen, or what was left of it, a pile of rubble. Ignoring upturned nails and shattered glass, splintered boards and crushed plaster, Poincie began to push, pull, and heave aside the rubble.

Eventually she saw Gatha's outstretched arm, and gradually uncovered her lifeless body. She must have been killed instantly by the collapse of an overhead beam. Poincie closed the eyelids and, with the leverage of a small plank, raised the beam from off the body. At about this time, she saw a shadow and looked up to see Bolt who had just arrived to check on them. Wordlessly, he lifted Gatha, placed her under the ackee tree and covered her with a sheet. They sat together with Bolt's arm around Poincie's shoulders, both blankly staring, not saying anything, both in shock.

Reverend Heath, haggard and disheveled, with dusty and mud-splattered dark clothes and shoes, joined them some time later, they knew not how long, time having become blurred and surreal.

Poincie cradled the frail, lifeless body of her beloved Aunt Gatha, and began to prepare her for burial. After giving her a sponge bath with water half-spilled from salvaged containers found in the rubble, she found fresh sheets from the clothesline that had fallen on the grass. These were to be the winding sheets that Gatha herself had described in one of the memories she had shared with Poincie.

Meanwhile, Bolt, rolling up his sleeves, had set about digging a grave at a shaded spot in the backyard as designated by Reverend Heath. When these duties were complete, they lowered her body into her resting place. The reverend kissed a scarlet stole which he placed on his shoulders and which hung down the front of his robes on either side, and with his voice quivering at times, performed the burial rites. They all, shovels and a spade in hand, completed the task. Bolt held a sobbing Poincie afterwards, saying nothing as she wept like Magdalene. Gatha was laid to rest in the only true home she had ever known.

Later, as they gathered their wits, they realized that the rectory, having been of sturdier construction, and located on higher ground above High Street, had not fared as badly as some of the other houses, but was still badly damaged, gaping cracks evident everywhere and doors jammed. Reverend Heath had had to reach the back of the premises by the side gate, the front door denying him access. They resolved to camp out in the yard until it was determined if the house was salvageable.

CHAPTER TWENTY-NINE

Aftershocks

Jack Hart surveyed the devastation that was Stokes Hall. His cottage was damaged beyond repair, as was the Bradfords'. The great house had withstood the ravages of the hurricane but succumbed to the earthquake. There were a few stone walls still standing to remind the onlooker that a grand residence once stood there, but the house was in shambles. Ironically, the slave quarters suffered little damage in comparison, because huts and wood houses rolled with the flow of the quake, flexed to accommodate the massive stressors, much like the residents of those humble dwellings.

The slaves were quietly moving about in a collective daze, rummaging among the ruins of the great house, extricating the bodies of the unfortunate, assisting as best they could those injured, laying them out on the grass and using ripped clothing to bind limbs, potions and poultices to salve wounds. Near slave quarters, some field laborers set to digging graves while females salvaged winding sheets to prepare the victims for burial. It all seemed surreal, like a nightmare with no imminent resolution. Jack observed all this, grateful that they needed no overseer to direct them, no backra to give orders. One remonstrated, "Massa Jack! Yu still here! Tenk Massa God. Yu alive!"

Soon Jack saw in the distance the approach of a horse and rider coming up the road toward what was left of the great house. It proved to be an English officer in the usual red tunic with the white criss-crossed sashes. The rider dismounted, led his horse over to where Jack was standing, and the men introduced themselves.

"Mr. Hart, I assume you are in charge here?"

"Yes, Lord Stokes is currently...."

"That's what I came about. It's bad news, I'm afraid. Lord Stokes died in the collapse of the Governor's Mansion in Port Royal."

Jack shook his head in disbelief as if in initial denial while he processed this news. "And what of George Bradford and his wife? They were both at the Governor's Mansion too."

"Bradford's body was found half-buried in the sand and silt some distance from the mansion, perhaps dragged there when the tidal wave came ashore and withdrew, taking much of the earthquake wreckage with it. Mrs. Bradford's body has not been found but we presume that she, like some 2,000 others, is dead. The quake took two thirds of Port Royal and buried it below the waves."

"Also, a house servant named Poincie was also in Port Royal for a visit. Do you have any news of her?"

"No information regarding her. I must warn you. There was widespread looting in Port Royal, and you can expect the same here. If you require added protection we can assign a limited number of militia, but everyone is in a similar state of desperation more or less. The quake caused extensive damage all over the island, especially to rigid stone structures including many churches."

"I believe we can manage here for the time being. I notice that the number of slaves has dwindled. I expect some slaves have escaped, while others have nowhere to go. I suppose I will get instructions soon from Robert Long and his law firm who are executors of this estate."

"And what will you do?"

"I...I don't know. All this news is a bit of a shock, as you can imagine. I just don't know...."

"Good luck! I must be on my way to the nearby estates."

The rider mounted his horse and departed, leaving Jack feeling suddenly alone. What to do next? Feeling vulnerable. Stokes dead. Bradford dead. Poincie probably dead. And if perchance she was alive, she wanted nothing to do with him anyway....Where to go next? Stay here, be the next overseer? Be like Bradford? No. Return to England, to the disgrace of having achieved nothing, to suffer the quiet disdain of his family? No future in Liverpool. That was clear before the departure from home. A dream shattered. Never return to England without having gained a fortune and established ascendance above the older brother.

Spurned by Poincie, belittled by Bradford, derided by even the slaves behind his back. What would he amount to? He didn't belong here. He couldn't become what was expected of him here or back in England. And the glory days of piracy were over. No future. No light at the end of this dark tunnel. Nothingness awaited Jack Hart. Nothing.

The next day they found him, hanging from the last remaining beam in the roof of his cottage.

Sometime later, Richard Long arrived from Montego Bay to assess the situation at Stokes Hall. He had heard of Jack Hart's passing and had ascertained that he had been given a proper burial courtesy of a neighboring plantation owner who survived the earthquake. Long carried a foolscap folder that enclosed Hart's legal contract and a newly arrived letter from England addressed to Hart, such letters typically taking three months to arrive in Jamaica. He intended to assemble Hart's personal effects and, along with any wages due him, send these back to his family in England with a letter informing them of his passing.

After returning to Montego Bay, Long prepared to send the package on the next vessel bound for England. Just before sealing the package he, for the first time, inspected the letter. The envelope indicated it was from Jack's father. Long contemplated returning the letter undisturbed but pondered whether the contents might have some bearing on the present circumstance. He decided to open the letter. It read:

My Dear Jack,

Here's hoping this letter finds you in good health and in good courage. Your mother and I have been thinking of you and of the challenges one faces in a strange land and an unfamiliar climate. We have been praying that the Good Lord would keep you and one day return you to us having achieved the goal of establishing yourself in a good way that would do credit to yourself and the family. I, however, write this letter with a heavy heart. Indeed, I regretfully write to bear some rather somber news. Your brother has died of the plague, one of many outbreaks that have devastated much of England these past few years. He passed away only yesterday. Of course, his wife and their young daughter are now left behind to grieve his loss. Polly was always fond of you and always asked of your wellbeing when they dined with us.

I am sure that you are aware that as my only remaining heir, you now have some additional responsibilities. Your mother and I are well advanced in age and have lately not been able to manage the affairs of our estate. Modest though it may be, it has grown to a respectable size and is a secure source of income for the foreseeable future. Your brother has been the one conducting our business affairs and with his passing we need your presence here as soon as convenient. I am sure the law firm with whom you have a contract would understand this. Come home, son.

Most sincerely,

Your Mother and Father.

Richard Long wept. Jack! Jack! You poor fool! Don't you know suicide is a permanent solution to a temporary problem?

Late the next day, some bedraggled citizens of Port Royal huddling together for mutual protection and surveying the awful spectacle, spotted Reverend Heath with Poincie and John Bolt. The crowd surrounded them, quietly whimpering and still in shock from the onslaughts of both nature and the horrible dregs of humanity. Lewis Galdy, still shivering from shock, joined the bedraggled group cowering in fear and mutual helplessness. Reverend Heath lifted his hands to the heavens and raised his voice to address the Almighty. It was a long, solicitous prayer, expressing the bewilderment of the people and their resignation to the will of God. Heath spoke as much to God as to the people. He would bring comfort by reflecting their feelings and venting their uncertainties. When he was finished, Lewis Galdy approached.

"Reverend... St. Paul's. It's all gone. Reduced to a pile of rubble!"

"Yes, my son. God chose not to spare it."

"But Reverend, the people need St Paul's, especially at a time like this."

"Yes, my son. But what can we do? The Lord giveth and the Lord taketh..."

"We must rebuild Reverend. We must!"

"Too soon to talk about that Lewis. So much devastation, so many ruined lives."

"We...er I, need a new beginning Reverend. I don't know what becomes of me now, but promise me that St Paul's will be rebuilt."

"We will see as time goes on what is to be the fate of St Paul's, indeed of Port Royal. And Lewis?"

"Yes, Reverend."

"Don't lose too much sleep over your situation. Many of your accusers are no more, and from all I can see, there's a good chance that witnesses will be hard to come by after this horrible disaster. Besides, I know John White quite well. He's the president of the Colonial Council. If he is still alive, I will put in a good word for you."

"Thank you, Reverend."

As Galdy turned and walked away, Heath once again surveyed the devastation around him, now mercifully shrouded in the gathering dusk. Houses built on sand indeed. No, a system built on sand. It cannot stand. Slavery, exploitation, abuse of God's creation, class warfare, it cannot stand. Port Royal was an artificial construct built on greed, arrogance, and an inflated sense of privilege and entitlement. All such entities come to an inevitable end when the pervasive sense of justice and fair play asserts itself through the efforts of man, the revulsion of nature, or a combination of both. How soon would this truism be felt by the rest of Jamaica? Did not those inland feel the shakings of that catastrophe? Did they not feel the rumblings of revolution? No, Mr. White. This was not a mere tremor that would soon pass. This was an earthshaking harbinger of change. "Every day the bucket goes to the well. One day the bottom will fall out."

Lewis Galdy turned and looked back once more at the scene, and once more saw the trio of Reverend Heath, Poincie, and John Bolt. By this time he could no longer see their faces but recognized their clothing. Reverend Heath, his black clerical robes gently fluttering in the breeze, had gathered under each arm both Bolt in his usual shade of green and Poincie in the gold frock Gatha had made for her. They walked away arm-in-arm toward higher ground as a new moon ascended behind them.

EPILOGUE

Today, a person watching the generally placid water lapping the shoreline at Port Royal would be unaware that buried beneath those gentle waves lie numerous stories of the lives, dreams, and ambitions of aristocrat and commoner, nobleman and brigand, freedman and slave. Beneath those waves lies a city, the most intriguing marine archaeological site in this hemisphere and perhaps the world. The ocean is a keeper of secrets, but plans are underway to return Port Royal to some semblance of the glory it once knew. Above the water, a new cruise ship terminal and resort are possibilities for development, while below an underwater museum is envisioned, complete with an underwater restaurant and facilities for the visitor. Perhaps Port Royal will once again rise to prominence as a hub of international activity, and this time on a more stable social, physical, and economic foundation. If this novel contributes in some small way to the realization of that dream, the effort would have been worth it.

ACKNOWLEDGEMENTS

Successful completion of this work was not possible without the assistance of some individuals for whose advice and feedback I am truly grateful. My wife Dalila and my son Sean provided valuable insights at all stages of this effort. I am also indebted to my lifelong friend and colleague Marjorie St. Rose, a professor of English at the College of the Bahamas and also to my colleague and friend at San Bernardino Valley College Professor Joel Lamore. The advice of these two individuals was significant in the shaping of this narrative. The counsel and encouragement of my sister Dr. Jannette Alexander was also pivotal in the completion of this effort. To all these individuals I express my sincere appreciation.

ABOUT THE AUTHOR

Horace Alexander was born in Kingston and grew up in Christiana, Jamaica. He holds a doctorate (Ed.D.) in Leadership and Administration and has been a school principal, district superintendent, college dean and college vicepresident. More recently he has been an English professor at San Bernardino Valley College in San Bernardino, California. He resides with his wife Dalila in Loma Linda, California. Dr. Alexander enjoys acoustic guitar, an exotic pen collection, and car restorations. In October 2010 he was inducted as a Lifetime Member of the Rolls Royce Foundation and currently serves as Chair of the Board of Directors of the Jamaica Cultural Alliance in Los Angeles. *Moon Over Port Royal* is his first novel.

64271290R00191

Made in the USA
Lexington, KY
02 June 2017